The LSO
Scenes from Orchestra Life

Eight o'clock, Leningrad – Patrick Hooley

On tour with the orchestra, Vienna

The LSO
Scenes from Orchestra Life

Linda Blandford

with photographs by
Suzie Maeder

Michael Joseph
London

For Douglas Cummings

This book was designed and produced by
The Oregon Press Limited, Faraday House,
8 Charing Cross Road, London WC2H 0HG

First published in Great Britain by
Michael Joseph Limited,
44 Bedford Square, London WC1 1984

Printed by Battley Brothers Ltd,
London SW4 0JN
Bound by Robert Hartnell Ltd,
Bodmin, Cornwall PL31 1EG

Design: Laurence Bradbury

Blandford, Linda
    The LSO.
    1. London Symphony Orchestra
    I. Title
    785'. 06'2421   ML286.8.L52L6
ISBN 0-7181-2463-4

Also by Linda Blandford: *Oil Sheiks: The Quest
For the New Arab* and *America on Five Valium a
Day*

Contents

1: First Meetings

It is often said that of the four London orchestras, the LSO is the most American in character. Whether or not this is intended as a compliment, depends on who says it. To one, it means that the orchestra has attack and brilliance; to another, that it is raffish and superficial. Is it ever that straightforward? All orchestras are as alike as they are different. They exist only at a distance, on a concert platform and as an ideal. Up close, they break down into the fragments of a hundred lives, talents and off-days.

The London Symphony Orchestra lists 84 playing members: 49 string players, 12 winds, 4 French horns, 9 brass and assorted others including harp, timpani, percussion and keyboard. (Horns are talked of separately: they are neither wind nor brass, yet they are both.) Sixty players might walk out on stage or as many as one hundred and ten. But whoever plays – members, associate members, first call extras, hopefuls, freelancers or just tired old availables – the whole is always 'The London Symphony Orchestra', and is judged as such.

It is a warm Sunday afternoon in early spring and Borough High Street in south-east London is closed. Around the corner in Trinity Church Square, orchestra trucks and cars surround the Henry Wood Hall (joint props: the London Philharmonic and London Symphony Orchestras). Downstairs in the dark crypt, sloppy cups of coffee stand on long tables. The regular poker players are in residence. Over here there is news of a great shot with a number five iron. Over there, a lament about the gate that wasn't fixed, the roof that wasn't mended and the wife who had had her say about both. Some men swap stories, impeccably paced and timed; years of practice go into them. Others rush to the telephones, full fat diaries in hand. There are ten minutes until the rehearsal downbeat. It is just another Sabbath day for the London Symphony Orchestra.

This morning it was Revenge of the Jedi in London NW8; this afternoon and evening, it is Tchaikovsky in SE1: a long weekend and the weariness shows. Above the plates of watery brown meat and sticky white rice, there is a sense at best of resignation, at worst of boredom. Another day, another session, another canteen. A few still have enough interest, or perhaps merely a sense of the absurd, to catch up on the morning's music reviews. Some things make a musician really happy: a full house, a standing ovation and un-adulterated praise next day. The LSO has been a bit thin on all of these of late.

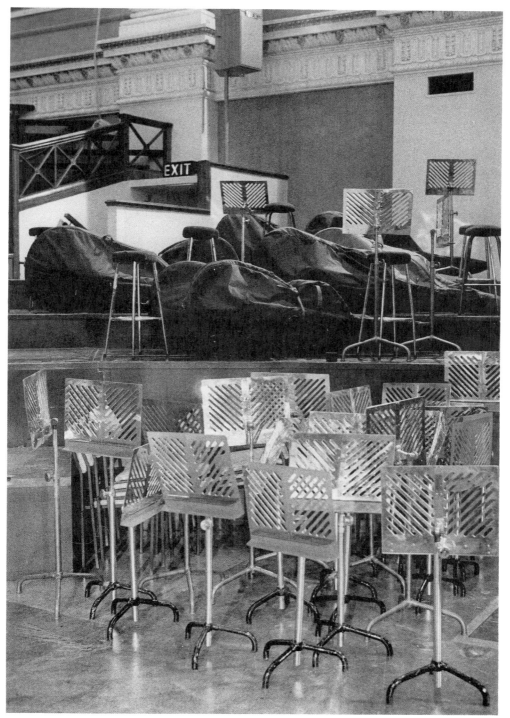

Town Hall, Birmingham

Critics are heartless beasts, lightly tossing off remarks about 'lack of inspiration', 'another ragged lacklustre performance' and complaints that 'deeper meanings were not revealed'. Or so it seems to those on the receiving end. Everyone loves a good review; everyone resents a bad one. Music as the idealization of man's highest yearnings is all very well for those who do not spend nine hours a day pursuing it, blowing, scraping, bowing and tonguing, self-employed and overworked. How hard to come to the great symphonic works as a player: the sheer problem of making the sound, strings that go flat, reeds that won't speak, muscles that ache. Who will sit out there making allowances for colds, headaches, sick children, grumbling parents or just the distraction of days spent in the car rushing between engagements.

An orchestra is reviewed as an entity as if it were in possession of one heart and one soul. It is no more and no less than the sum total of its players at any given moment. The musicians in the crypt here this afternoon are an unprepossessing lot. Some are messy, paunchy, hair awry. Others in ties have a stab at that odd formality that Englishmen go in for when they are trying to keep up standards. Most have the unhealthy pallor that comes with a bad diet and not enough fresh air. All they have in common is that they live with the constant contradiction between trying to make a living and, at the same time, trying to keep within them enough vulnerability to make music at its highest and most intense level. Not surprisingly, music sometimes loses.

It is two thirty. Someone somewhere is giving the call: 'Gentlemen, please'. The crowd dissolves. Upstairs Tchaikovsky is to be given his chance. So too is the conductor of the day, Yuri Simonov, chief conductor of the Bolshoy Opera, a People's Artist of the USSR and here by courtesy of Goskoncert, Moscow's unpredictable cultural agency.

Simonov comes from a system that looks after its own. The favoured enjoy both material blessings and a nurturing security. The musicians seated before him enjoy no security that is not of their own making and, as freelance members of the LSO, their material blessings for rehearsal and concert are about £50 each. Simonov is a middle fee conductor, about £1500, so this week of concerts is worth perhaps £6000 to him, or at least to Goskoncert. It is, in some ways, a very strange situation. As the LSO's only shareholders, its playing members hire the conductor to do their bidding. As orchestra musicians it is they who must do his. He has but three rehearsals in which, so common lore has it, to forge of this disparate group an instrument for his personal musical vision. As conductor, he makes no sound and yet must achieve, through the muscles and nerve endings of the players before him, a performance that can seem to be of his making.

He has few weapons at his disposal. In the old days of the musical martinets, a conductor could play the tyrant, scold, wasp or shrew at his will, but not in these democratic times. Besides, in that grey haze of overwork, who can take all that stuff seriously any more? The London musical scene is no nursery; tantrums, the stock-in-trade of yesteryear's conductor, have a way of looking very silly now. Simonov has before him a group of jaded, seen-it-all-before musicians who would turn against him at one false word. They have seen the young whippersnappers with their immaculate stick technique and cocky ways, the pompous old hacks clinging to an international prestige for which they once seemed destined, the middle-aged who have not quite made it trying to smarm their way into favour. They have betrayed them all in their own inimitable LSO fashion.

It seems at times as if, of the four London orchestras (London Philharmonic, London Symphony, Philharmonia, Royal Philharmonic), the LSO has the least professional pride in playing well for its own sake. If it can give of its best it is as capable of the opposite. In rehearsal, an orchestra's teeth are quickly bared. The musicians talk too much, they play on long after the request to stop, they wilfully misunderstand suggestions as to phrasing or attack. Anarchy is ever close to the surface. Musical authority is an intangible quality, not automatically linked to talent, intelligence or experience. Quite simply, players, like dogs and children, know who has it and who does not.

It is not clear as Simonov comes in, black cardigan knotted over his tiny shoulders, pretty young interpreter trotting behind, how, if at all, he will express such authority. First impressions are not promising. An interpreter is a crutch; musical markings whether in Italian, German or whatever, are universally understood. And, in any case, singing a phrase expresses more than any amount of words. Besides, Simonov is very short with very long black hair – an immediate mark against a conductor suggesting, as it does, a deadly combination of vanity and over-assertiveness. He has a pinched and moody face. Musicians who spend a lifetime examining and responding to the gallery of faces that pass before them have learned to read every such sign.

Simonov, however, gathers up the core of the rehearsal from the start. He jumps energetically onto the podium: it is a silent but emphatic declaration and recognized as such. 'I am not afraid of you,' it says. 'I am looking forward to working but beware – I am much fresher and tougher than you are.' Musicians, shambling and uncoordinated as they may appear offstage, have a finely tuned and sophisticated understanding of body language. This orchestra in particular likes to take its cues from colleagues, not from the man above them. Subtle gestures come to take the place of words. Players learn to hear, to listen, to read one another with an animal-like acuity. Friend and foe alike can be recognized at a distance; there is no place here for pretence.

Watch, for instance, today's leader, Ashley Arbuckle, sitting back comfortably in his chair. His posture is that of a solid man, at ease with himself and his station in life. His hair style is another clue, careful, perfectly arranged. It is the hair style of a leader who will never play his heart out in his solos – it is not his way – but he will always be there, always be prepared and he will never get lost. The wild man is not in his soul. He is dependable down to his well-polished brown boots. All of this, Simonov too, knows in an instant. It shows in the way the conductor turns to him to discuss bowings, never talking over him to the first violin section at large as he might elsewhere. Arbuckle responds to this bit of flattery and, in return, quickly claps his hands for order when whispering creeps restlessly around the chairs.

Musicians' sensitivities are the same the world over. Simonov shows his respect for them in small but telling ways. The violins are having a spot of bother with their pizzicati. This is a player's problem, not easy to deal with. A conductor is traditionally allowed to say almost anything to the strings, the orchestra's lumpen proletariat, but a 'pizz' is a unique colouristic contribution, and no other instrument can even approximate it. This is personal territory. Simonov steps down for a quiet word with Arbuckle, an indication that he is not giving orders but asking advice. A quick conference and it is the leader who turns to his colleagues with suggestions. Pluck much louder, perhaps, and closer to the bridge to make a sharper sound? The orchestra plays on.

The bassoons are bothering Simonov; he wants more excitement, more vehemence and intensity in this phrase. The bassoons do not feel exciting at this moment. Nor do the trombones, next in line for Simonov's special attention. Is it chance that he has picked on two of this orchestra's most independent-minded sections? At the best of times, trying to tell a wind or brass player how to phrase something is asking for trouble. These are not rank-and-file, backstand string players to be told what to do: wind and brass players are soloists, with the soloist's mentality. Talk of balance is one thing, but a musical judgment is another. Simonov does not back down; he rubs his points home, sings the phrases, asks for them again and again. But then, through the interpreter, he asks the players to go home and work it out themselves. In an instant, he has handed them back their self-respect. Now the orchestra is paying attenion: heads, backs and arms come up, eyes open wider. Simonov was angry, but it was the right kind of anger it seems. Crucially, he was man enough to drop it in time. He senses the surge of energy before him, born of this scene; he pounces on it, conducting with arms flailing as if now he can ask for anything.

Tchaikovsky poured his tortured life into his music. No wonder that those who must re-create it are quick to offence, to laughter, to resentment. This music runs gut deep. But Simonov wants it all; he will not settle for some rough and scrappy run through. He is asking the orchestra to play out, to dig into the strings, attack and phrase with passion. His big, generous gestures demand a response. With his face and his body, he lives out the drama of the symphony, and amazingly the players react in kind. The LSO can infuriate but it can also astound. Its greatness comes through now. There is an almost reckless abandon in its brilliance, all the more astonishing because with this high emotional temperature comes even more accurate playing. When this

Ashley Arbuckle

excitement is generated, it affects everyone together: no dead wood in the backstands now. Few orchestras in the world can respond so immediately and so in kind. Suddenly, half an hour feels like a few minutes.

Tired and worn down as they are by twenty-two hours of film recording in the last two days, these musicians long for the purge of splendid music-making. They long to be moved, to lose themselves in the emotion of the moment. It is what sustains them through the constant scramble for work and money. It is, after all, why they became musicians in the first place. It is, also, why many of them will pass a lifetime in an orchestra that cannot guarantee their daily bread and, at most, promises the hope of a daily grind, year after year. For this moment of forgetfulness they will love Simonov – for the time being, at any rate. It is a love affair; there have been many such affairs in the past, but some last longer than others.

While the lush and swollen phrases of Tchaikovsky well upstairs, life goes on in the darkened crypt. At the canteen counter, long lines of tea cups are being marshalled for the break. More supplies of sticky buns are being called up. In one corner, John Duffy, the orchestra's personnel manager, pores over his endless lists: an extra couple of horns needed here, a cello to deputize there. He tuts and mutters as he goes through the release request forms. A bassoon has to miss this rehearsal, first oboe does not want to play that concert. The oboe is the soul of an orchestra, the prima donna among the wind soloists; he is the first to be missed, the hardest to replace.

This scene is ironic, really, for the LSO was formed in 1904 by a group of players reacting against Henry Wood's dictat that there would be no more deputies in his orchestra. Now the question of who will play this and who will stand in for that is the bane of Duffy's orderly life. Will Simonov notice, for instance, when the co-principal cello is missing tomorrow afternoon?

There is a sudden intrusion in the crypt's peaceful hour. Simonov is summoning the librarian upstairs. There is a mistake in the parts. Of course there is a mistake in the parts. No one can remember when Tchaikovsky's Manfred symphony was last played by this orchestra. If there is only one bad spot, that will be a mercy. From a small, windowless room in a corner of the crypt, Henry Joseph Greenwood emerges silently padding towards the stairs, head bowed, long arms hanging by his side. 'Flannel foot', as the stage managers call him, looks every inch the devoted but resigned family retainer brought forth to meet his master's disapproval. He soon returns, his long white face as impenetrable as ever. Conductors. To serve them is both his joy and his curse. 'Conductors', he says, 'can cause one a lot of internal displeasure.'

The library in the crypt is Henry Greenwood's private empire. The patches of patterned carpet that cover the cold, tiled floor, he bought himself one afternoon at a Wembley street market. His personal coffee maker stands on a table. But there is more to it than that. Fifteen years of his cataloguing and tidying have left their mark on the orchestra's legacy of music. 'I do feel that a little bit of me lingers over the LSO library', he says. This is where it begins – with the bare notes written on the page. The greatest of those who wrote them are long dead. Books and scores show reproductions of their original manuscripts. 'It is', as Henry says, 'Just a little bit hair-raising really. These people are legendary and for a moment you feel almost in touch with them.'

Not that he has much time for the poetry of the music in his job. By the door stand parcels neatly wrapped in brown paper. Some Grieg has to go back to Danish radio; there are Rodrigo guitar concertos for Peer Musikverlag, Hamburg; Mussorgsky tone poems for Casa Musicale Sonzogno di Pero Ostali, Milan; something already forgotten for Editions Salabert in France. He must hunt down everything that is to be played, make sure that it arrives in time and then send it off again across the world. At the moment his days are haunted by Mozart's little-known mass, the Waisenhausmesse in C, K 139. Claudio Abbado, the orchestra's principal conductor, starts rehearsing it next week. Who would have thought that Mozart could give Henry so much trouble? He is always ready for it with the South American composers ('their music is always hard to find. It's mostly been handwritten and duplicated on poor paper – very dodgy, very dodgy'). But not Mozart, surely?

Bahrenreiter in Kassel was able to produce a score. Breitkopf & Hartel in Wiesbaden said it had parts. These took a month to arrive and when he unwrapped the parcel, the poor librarian found only string parts inside. Time went by and the anxious Henry threw himself upon the good services of the orchestra's multilingual harpist to put in a stern call to Wiesbaden. Last week two oboe parts and an organ part turned up in the post. Still missing is the music for two oboes, four trumpets and three trombones. How tempting it must be for Henry to photocopy Bahrenreiter's highly copyrighted score to send out to his faithful band of copyists. They could then write out the missing parts at £2 a page just in time for him to drive to his favoured copying service, Presto ('they're very sensible about music. They always leave margins a little wider on the outside edge for when it gets tatty'). Somehow on the stands next week, the music will greet the players as if none of all this had happened. Another narrow call. A stiff letter will be in the post to Breitkopf & Hartel. 'I think it will make hardly any difference', says the librarian with the gloom of one used to the arcane world of music publishing.

Perhaps it would not have been so bad if Henry had had the prospect of a recording to console him, so that all this work would take its place in posterity. A rare gem on a concert schedule usually suggests the ghostly presence of a recording company. But, alas, it is not to be. In the bound score of all the Mozart masses lying open on Henry's desk – his crib, so to speak, lent to him by Abbado – there is an inscription: 'Milan '74. In hope of a beautiful recording, yours Rainer'. It did not take Henry long to decipher that. Rainer Brock produces Abbado's records for Deutsche Grammophon, the company with which the conductor has an exclusive contract. Abbado did his Waisenhausmesse quite a long time ago with the Vienna Philharmonic; it just took ten years for him to get round to playing it again. Thousands and thousands of pounds worth of soloists' fees, weeks and weeks of work to track down the music – and not even a recording at the end of it. It is enough to make anyone sigh.

It would, of course, be Abbado that gave this latest patch of trouble to the relentless bloodhound in the library. Abbado is Henry's nemesis: ('He means well – God help him'). On Henry's shelves are huge packets of what he calls 'Abbadoized parts'. He runs something of a cottage industry these days shipping out these packets to the Chicago Symphony and the Vienna Philharmonic, Abbado's other main orchestras. Despite all the grumbling, he is obviously not displeased to be thus at the centre of international musical affairs. Musicians love a good grumble and, like Henry, often use it to cover affection.

'There was a time', laments Henry, 'when conductors just took the music as it came for the most part. Now we have Abbado who rescores things more than anyone in the world. He'll decide the cellos sound a bit weak there and that the second bassoon or third horn can double on it. Once a set of parts has been adjusted to his needs, it's no use to anyone else.' What Henry hates most are the long, detailed letters that arrive in the post sent from whichever hotel room around the world the conductor happens to find himself in. 'Oh Abbado's handwriting is awful stuff,' he shakes his head despairingly. Occasionally on tour he sees the Italian coming purposefully towards him and his heart sinks. 'He wants instruments to double and I have to copy the extra music into the parts. No rehearsal afterwards, nothing. It takes hours to write and it could all be wrong.' It never has been, of course. 'In Edinburgh once, when the LSO was playing *Carmen*, I actually went out between acts and crawled through the opera pit to copy things into the cello parts. I swear he looks at the score and if he sees someone has eight bars' rest, he can't bear to think of them just sitting there.'

Nowadays it is the fashion for music to be played in the 'original', that is with all the later editing, rescoring and embellishments removed. Another of Henry's trials has to do with the newly reissued editions of Beethoven, Mozart and Haydn. 'These parts are so bare', complains Henry, 'that they're unplayable as they are, so you've got to write in bowings for the strings and put back all the expression marks. By the time you've finished they're just like the old parts that have been derided for being so over-edited.' Abbado is very much in the forefront of today's conductor-musicologists trying to be faithful to the composer's written note and intention. And yet here in Henry's library is the evidence that nothing is simple, that the note and the intention may not necessarily seem synonymous. At least the librarian knows by now what Abbado is after, trying always to strengthen and to thicken the musical line. Little of *his* music-making escapes his amanuensis in the small, fluorescent-lit room.

Indeed, the librarian is an orchestra's musical confessor. He knows who hasn't taken home parts to practise for twenty years and who always goes off with something. 'Roy Jowitt, the principal clarinet, practises a lot – and he never bends the parts either.' High praise indeed. What Henry most hates is a player who abuses the music for which he cares with such loving respect. 'One of our first violins is very rough. It looks as if he's marked his parts with a tarbrush on the end of a stick.' He knows when a rehearsal has gone well and when it has gone badly. The markings in the music tell all to the one who has had to read and repair them. Difficult, modern music comes in for a special share of heavy, ugly pencil scrapings all over it.

But conductors are Henry Greenwood's forte. When he sees their own scores so that he can mark up the orchestra parts before rehearsals, he soon sees how well they know the music. When they have to mark in a triangle to remind themselves to beat in three, it does not go unnoticed. 'Sometimes they mark them up such a lot, they're even shy for me to see them.' He reserves his special approval for those few conductors to whom he gives good marks for clarity, such as Sir Colin Davis and Rafael Kubelik. 'There was an old school of conductors and it hasn't been passed on really – Bruno Walter, Furt-wängler. Kubelik is one of the last of the breed, he has absolute competence. When they've lived a long time and they've thought it all out, they know exactly what they want. They don't "feel" their way through it.

'You see, the more you look at composers' scores, the more you realize what an insight they've had and what great craftsmanship. They were very talented people really. I remember when I went to see Beethoven's house in Bonn, it was desperately touching and very sad. They fought against such odds, they left a legacy for millions to enjoy and yet they had such bloody awful lives themselves. It seems so unfair. With all my problems, compared to them, my life's been a bed of roses.'

2: On a Monday Morning

The 'Sold' sign is still up outside the terraced house in Kilburn in north-west London. Until a few weeks ago it was a lodging house and each room has its old, decrepit gas cooker. There is dry rot, rising damp, dangerous wiring and a sagging roof. It is barely livable in now and will be worse when the builders arrive. It would require a real optimist to look at this tumbledown house and see the cosy family home that is meant to come to pass if and when Paddy and his men finish the work.

In what passes for the back kitchen, Sue Mallet is engaged in the daily struggle of breakfast with her 3-year-old daughter, Aroona. Toast to be eaten, trousers to be unearthed somewhere upstairs, teeth to be cleaned. Sue's husband, a freelance oboe player, has already left for a recording session. It is nearly nine and Aroona has still to be driven through the West Hampstead traffic jams to spend the day with Margaret the baby minder. 'People always say "How do you do your job and have a family?" It's easier than you think,' says Sue with that cheerful enthusiasm for which she is legendary over telephones around the world.

Sue Mallet is the LSO's artistic administrator and the incarnation of a heroine in a schoolgirl story, forever saving the day. She is the one who books concerts, conductors, soloists, tours, finds replacements, negotiates fees, charters planes, wafts the orchestra magically about the place and keeps within her head the million details of LSO life. 'It's barmy, isn't it? Peter Hemmings, our managing director, always says, "Sue, you're very good with lunatics but not so good with normal people." Still, I think *he's* an odd fish. I suppose you've got to be in his job – you've got to ponce around with all those city folk.'

She represents that side of the LSO that still cleaves to the ideal of the devoted amateur, to music as a calling. She is a reminder of those far-off days when the LSO was formed, of the players who gave concerts without a fee, of the conductors who gave theirs back when times were tight. A far cry from today. 'I'm still not entirely hardened by people being so mercenary' is the way she puts it. When she talks of the LSO as 'family', she means it. The orchestra will never be just another business to her. It seemed quite natural that she should take Aroona into the office with her for the first six months, perching her on the desk in a baby chair. They went together to meetings of the London Orchestral Board, which says much about the chummy nature of

Morning Break at the Henry Wood Hall – Graham Elliott talking to Francis Saunders

London musical life. George Mann, then head of the Festival Hall, would offer his private office when Aroona needed changing. Peter Diamand, formerly director of the Edinburgh Festival, then head of the Royal Philharmonic Orchestra, would pitch into weighty matters of the yearly budget while bouncing Aroona on his knee. The very picture would surely horrify them in New York, Berlin or Vienna.

The LSO started as a do-it-yourself operation and that spirit pervades it still. But as things get tougher, and the sums involved get ever higher, it is changing. 'One of the arts in this business', says Sue, 'is covering your tracks the whole time. I always make sure that if something goes wrong, I'm covered by a memo to the board. That's the way to survive in London orchestras. If you don't, one wouldn't last very long. Surviving, that's all it is.'

She drives her car into the Barbican garage. It is after ten and her office phone is already ringing: Athens, Paris, Chicago, confirmations, cancellations, queries, dates that might open up, others that have fallen through. There is a discrepancy somewhere between this young woman, living and working on a shoestring, and the glamorous, moneyed image of international classical music.

Just along the corridor from Sue's office, a sandy-haired Australian is wryly examining the latest computer print-out bringing the bad news of ticket sales from the Barbican box office. The Barbican Hall, official home of the LSO since March 1982, holds 2000. The print-out tells the by now familiar story: 1872 tickets available for this concert, yet more for that. Bruce Campbell, the LSO's accountant, has another week of juggling tricks. 'Nearly 80 years of history and the orchestra has nothing, no capital, nothing,' he says. 'If we were a normal company, we'd be out of business by now.'

It is a tale common to every cultural organization in the land, and many more besides. The LSO has a cash flow problem. When everyone did the figures for the Barbican in 1978-9, they were based on a minimum 70 per cent capacity audience. This was a conservative estimate, or so it seemed in those balmy days when the LSO's concerts at the Royal Festival Hall were over 80 per cent full. The orchestra committed itself to playing at the Barbican three months a year and to filling that hall every night during those months with some form of music. Its first month was a triumph. Afterwards, was it that the novelty of coming to the great concrete slab in the City of London began to wear off? Or was it only the recession biting deeper? Whatever the reasons, the audiences quickly dropped. On every concert that it plays there, the LSO now loses £2000.

In one form or another (the Arts Council, the Greater London Council and the City Corporation), the orchestra receives nearly a million pounds a year in subsidies and still runs at a loss. In its list of priorities, the players are always paid first. 'We've been a few days late with their cheques once or twice but that's all.' Outsiders, such as conductors and soloists, must wait, although some of the more ruthless have been known to demand cash on the night with the tacit threat that without it they will not walk out on stage. There is a £250,000 overdraft at the bank and half as much again owing elsewhere. 'I wake up in the middle of the night worrying about it all,' says Campbell. But, Micawber-like, the orchestra believes that something will always turn up. And it always does, for the players at least. In the last two years, they have been engaged to record the soundtrack for more than 20 films. Last year alone, the players took home between them £700,000 from film sessions and the 'orchestra' made a 10 per cent management fee on that. Besides, the LSO may owe money to others but its own debtors owe something too. 'Paying late is the British malaise', says the Australian with a sigh. No wonder that the orchestra members, all too aware, agreed to play over 600 three-hour sessions last year. There are those who call it greed; survival is the word they use a lot around the LSO these days.

But, somehow, no one doubts that it will all be all right: it always has been. There has never been a time in the orchestra's history that it has not had to worry about money. This is just a little bit worse than usual.

On the other side of the mighty Barbican complex, a world away from the cares of money, a small group of natural allies are getting together in the Cockpit Theatre. This morning, the semi-finals are being held of the annual Shell-LSO scholarship for young players. This year it is the turn of the brass. It should be a tense moment: young players from all over Britain are competing not only for the first prize of £3000 but for the honour of being singled out by the LSO. Top musical talent is rare and a major orchestra likes to know where it is, for there lies the future.

If this were a string or piano competition, the atmosphere might indeed be deadly. Students of those instruments are weaned on the solo repertoire; they learn later how to be not stars but colleagues. From the beginning, brass players work with others. The comradeship of the group is what sustains them. There is also the fact that a brass instrument is new and, in the scheme of things, relatively cheap. It is hard to have the kind of relationship with a trumpet that a violinist can dream of experiencing with a great Cremonese fiddle. For the brass player, the instrument is merely a tool, representing only a small part of a musical contribution. Raw talent is here more nakedly on display.

As far as most audiences are concerned, an orchestra is the strings punctuated by a few solos in the winds; the brass is something that just growls or blows away in the back, mostly in the loud bits. Some conductors, it is true, treat the brass and winds alike as the orchestra's lieutenants, and one or two (notably Solti and Szell in his time) hardly ever look at the strings; they conduct almost entirely to the winds and brass. But, by and large, the brass must look to one another for comfort. The cut-and-thrust of competition is not in their natures. So, if this morning does, in the end, yield a winner, that must be laid aside for the moment. Essentially, this is a workshop and on hand are some of the LSO's principals to tackle some of the knotty problems of projection, articulation or just of coming in on time.

To outsiders, 'the brass' may be lumped all together but each instrument bestows upon those who seek to master it something of its own character. The pyrotechniques, for instance, are mostly in the trumpet, so he will be the one with the dash and verve. The trombone is the brass's philosopher – even early on, the trombones in Mozart represented the hereafter, the ghost of the Commendatore in *Don Giovanni*. Lyrical solos are so difficult on a trombone that it takes almost a lifetime to learn to play them. To be able to do so with musicianship must make of a man a thinker. In the Brahms first symphony, the trombones sit there for three full movements before playing their first note, but when they do it is a solo of awesome, purplish colour, a moment of glory. 'What we do', says the LSO principal to one student, 'amounts most of the time, unfortunately, to a kind of musical navvying, but it's got to be a nice kind of navvying.' Only another trombone player would see the pride concealed behind that flat statement.

On comes John Fletcher, the LSO's principal tuba. Of one young man, he asks for the solo from Wagner's Ride of the Valkyries. When he shakes his head at the end, it is with sorrowful understanding. 'The late Bruno Walter, you know, said he'd give any job to the first man who could play that statement loud and clear with the right buoyant rhythm. Let's try it again.' As he listens, it is as if he is blowing every note with him. 'About five times a year you have to play a solo – and play it without dying,' he sympathizes at the end. Others may make free with jokes about Tubby the Tuba, but a tuba player knows how important is his contribution to his colleagues. If the one man on the bottom has a full, deep sound with really good intonation, it makes it easier for the whole orchestra to play in tune.

What comes through in these hours is the excitement of it all. To these young players with their experience of school bands and local orchestras, the LSO represents the height of their ambition. As they blow away on their solos and excerpts, all their youthful nerves and longing come through. Everything lies before them. It is both touching and a little sad. How many will still care at the end of a career as they do now at its beginning?

Jack Long's house in Woodside Park is very still. After the bustle of orchestra life, it is this absolute stillness that stands out. Occasionally a car goes by or Pepe, the Yorkshire terrier, leaps at the front window yapping at a passing stranger. It is clearly a house given over to the imposition of order: there is no clutter, no familiar old objects lie around. The carpet is lilac, the windows are covered with pretty nets. It is small and neat and nice. In the greenhouse, Mrs Long, white-haired, softly-spoken is potting some plants. Compared to

John Fletcher, *Barbican, London*

Jack's, her life has always seemed rather humdrum: the house, their two boys, the garden. After 46 years, it is odd to have a husband about the place. This has always been her territory as, in a way, were their sons.

Today marks the beginning of her husband's official retirement from the LSO. For twenty-five years, it was the orchestra that was his real home and the cello that was his companion. Woodside Park was very pallid stuff by comparison. But he always came back, however tired and grumpy. Outside, he was just another orchestra man. Here at home, he always came first. Mrs Long is not much of a concert goer, her arthritic hip gets in the way, but she has always understood that she married a first class musician. She has believed in his playing even when he has not. 'Oh Jack should have been a soloist', she says with simple pride. 'He could have been if he had wanted to – he played so beautifully.' In her kitchen, he is a great man.

But then she did not have to sit there during all those years listening to conductors, far younger and less experienced than he, carrying on as if he and his colleagues had never seen Beethoven, never played Brahms, much less noticed the markings in Mahler. Jack Long is 72; he has earned his living on the cello for over half a century. Those years have left him with a sharp tongue, a hint of bitterness. 'I've had more than one brush with conductors. I can be a bit vitriolic, as you can imagine. But I don't think there's one conductor I haven't played with except for Toscanini and I'm soured by drawing comparisons.' He made sure that his retirement was of his own making, that at least was in his control. He moved slowly back through the section, from first stand to almost last, from full membership of the LSO to associate. Now it is over. He will substitute when they need an extra body but he is no longer part of it. 'It has its moment of regret. I've been so used to getting in the car every morning and going off to Henry Wood and the Barbican and yet when I've got there I've thought "I've got six hours of this". And then I look up at the rostrum and think "Oh, and I've got six hours of that and all."'

The LSO is a restless orchestra, quickly bored and living always near the edge. Jack Long will have to get used to days that are the same, to small pleasures and a homely routine: visiting friends, walking the dog, driving his wife to the shops. It is probably more attention than he has had time to give her since they first courted all those years ago when he was playing in a Lyons tea shop orchestra. He feels he owes her the years ahead if only for all those in which she held the family together while the best of him went to that other family, the orchestra. 'Coming home when you're out playing all day, you're tired and your wife wants to tell you about her life and your children want to tell you their difficulties, but you have your own troubles. You come in and you're likely to settle yourself on the whisky bottle and then you're more absorbent. In the orchestra, you share your grumbles with the other players. So – and I'm sorry to say this when there's more years behind me than in front

Jack Long, *Manchester*

William Lang, *Sheffield*

– I enjoy my marriage more now. And I enjoy music more, too, because I'm
not playing for my bread and butter. It's all money; everything's money now.
As long as that diary is full up, they know they can pay the large mortgages,
the rates and rear their children. And life is slipping by. That's the tragedy.'

He is talking of himself too, of course. He has had a distinguished career,
but he will always wonder what more he might have done. He thinks now he
would have liked the life of a string quartet player: all that repertoire, all those
musical decisions, and he forgets what it would be like to be glued to three
other players. An apprenticeship in a major orchestra is one way for a cello
soloist to start a career, more so than for any other instrumentalist. Suppose
he too had followed that path? Might he have become another world soloist –
Gregor Piatigorsky, Leonard Rose, János Starker? And he forgets that he left
the London Philharmonic largely because he had tired of endless touring and
the LSO seemed to be more home-based in those earlier days. What he is
really picturing is not a career with more glamour, money or honour but a
dream in which he would somehow always have played at his best. 'It's hard
to play well when you're doing it nine hours a day,' as he says. Perhaps there
was not enough talent, perhaps there was. There were other considerations. 'I
wasn't pushing enough and I had to go and earn my living. I had a family to
keep. There are many fine musicians who would have had careers as soloists
but they had to dig themselves into an orchestra and that's why they've got so
disgruntled.'

The best years were the seven on the LSO's front stand with Kenneth
Heath: 'The enthusiasm with which the two of us set about playing on that
desk was wonderful. He wasn't too domineering, he realized that the man
sitting next to him also had ideas. But after he left, they brought in another
principal and that was a question of a partnership not working. From then on
I lost my appetite for being up there at the front. Being right at the back is
really an education: you can't hear what the conductor says, the messages
don't always come back. But I'll say one thing: wherever you sit you have to
be committed. When I look round sometimes, I'm cruel. When we started it
was an honour to play in an orchestra – you were a very particular person. It is
an artistic professon – it's not digging the road and some of them forget that.'

The bitterness, the cynicism do not go very deep. Somewhere still is the
shadow of the 6-year-old who played 'Rock of Ages' on an old cigar box with
a broom handle (his first cello) round the fire while his mother listened in
tears. He still thinks at times of that small boy in Salisbury, the grocer's son,
who went to the cathedral close for cello lessons ('Oh, the aroma of bees-
wax!'). Now a succession of small boys turn up every week on his North
London doorstep. 'I love teaching because you can pass on the tradition and
your corrected mistakes.' What he is also passing on is his love for music and
the instrument, the strongest he has ever known. 'I adore the cello – it's an
extension of yourself, you can pour all your love into it.'

Sometimes he stands at the window of the upstairs back bedroom that has been turned into his music studio, looks down over the row of empty gardens and listens on a little tape machine to some of his BBC recitals recorded many, many years ago. His wife was right; he did play beautifully. 'A sense of long line – it's like love, isn't it?' he says afterwards. And for all the complaints, he will miss the orchestra, the high moments, the concerts that go well. After twenty-five years, there is no pension, only an annuity payment and a nice letter from the LSO board.

'The comradeship, the understanding between the players of the LSO, that's what I really love. I do love the orchestra – it's as good as any now and better than most – but I left because I thought it was time. I'll say one thing, though – certain people are getting away with murder. I can't bear it, but I don't care now. They can do what they like with me. I've got the rest of my life in front of me – or what's left of it.'

3: On the Road

Washington, D.C.

Some months before the afternoon in question, a letter was despatched from the West 57th Street headquarters of Columbia Artists Management in New York. It was addressed to the sales manager of the Capitol Hilton Hotel in Washington. The wording was nicely judged, a fine mixture of supplication and veiled threat; 'Dear Debbie', it began in the warm American way. 'As you know, the world-famous LONDON SYMPHONY ORCHESTRA will be guests at your hotel during their up-coming 1983 American Tour. This prestigious Orchestra has traveled extensively throughout the world and is accustomed to the finest accommodations. We know we can count on you to select your rooms according to their standards.' On tour, evidently, an orchestra acquires an image that is not immediately recognizable to those at home.

At four o'clock on this hot, sunny Monday in Washington, the writer of this letter can reflect that he has much cause for satisfaction. As the doyen of American classical music road managers, Dennis Gargan has his own standards to keep up. He likes, for instance, that they still tell the story in the LSO about that famous time in Providence, Rhode Island, when the orchestra arrived to find not one restaurant open and only fifteen minutes left before the downbeat. As if by magic, Dennis located a tiny, out-of-the-way diner, charmed or press-ganged every customer into service and emerged just minutes later triumphantly bearing 120 sandwiches on a platter. That is the kind of challenge Dennis Gargan loves. 'Not to sound braggy,' he says, straightening his emerald trousers, opening wide his china-blue eyes and examining his polished Gucci loafers, 'but I work great under disaster.'

Dennis is nearly 50 and he has been doing this kind of thing for years: scuttling about New York to find a hundred umbrellas at seven in the morning to protect the delicate heads of the Scottish National Orchestra; rushing about Miami to collect enough bottles of mineral water for the entire Orchestre de Paris (and then beating his breast because he had forgotten bottle openers for each bedroom); opening temporary bank accounts, running to earth available swimming pools and doing it all with dazzling panache. Touring a modern-day orchestra has all the bravura of moving an old-fashioned circus. It is also as bulky, as complicated and makes about as much financial sense. Five weeks, seven countries (the United States, Australia, Japan, Hong Kong, Thailand, Singapore, Malaysia), 17 concerts

Waiting for luggage, Stanstead Airport

and £575,000 worth of costs: that's the London Symphony Orchestra's World Tour. It is a flourish of some sort, that much at least is clear.

Dennis is only nannying the LSO through its first eight days: six American cities, seven concerts; fee per concert $35,000 to $40,000. Simple maths suggests that no orchestra today can tour without someone putting up a huge sum of money, or losing it, or both. Dennis is not a big 'overview' man: his main preoccupation is his show, his performance. Soon the LSO plane, a £300,000 British Airways charter, will touch down at Dulles Airport outside Washington and Dennis will be 'on'. A cardboard box sits on his lap: 93 envelopes with 93 keys for the Capitol Hilton's best rooms (regular rate $130 a night, rate to the LSO, $45 – another Gargan coup). Standing by in the Hilton lobby are six bellboys, inspected, briefed and tipped, ready to receive and sort hundreds of pieces of LSO luggage that must then be delivered to the correct rooms. Gerry, the driver from Gainsville, Georgia – unexpectedly free after a nine months' road tour of *Annie* – has already arrived at the airport. He drove up this morning with a 40 foot truck trailer rented from a small firm in New Jersey – another Gargan price break. It will be Gerry's job to collect the instruments from the plane and drive them to a guarded loading bay beneath the Kennedy Center. 'Classical stuff like this is a bit chintzy but it's almost like a vicarious career for me,' says Gerry. 'When I do this kind of work I'm in my element – I'm an entertainer myself, I play the accordion.' Buses await the musicians, a long black limousine is on hold for the conductor. There is almost nothing that Dennis has not planned for, no detail too small for his attention. As Dennis always says, 'you're only as good as your last performance.'

On the way to the airport in the conductor's limousine (an LSO expense), Dennis gets some bad news from on high. He is to be sent back to New York to watch over the Monteverdi Choir for a night. A quick frown and then Dennis smiles bravely through. He too is an artist and that is what happens when you are in demand. It is curious how often those on the periphery of the music world acquire the very characteristics of 'the artist' that performers themselves are so often eager to lose. The supporting players grow ever more mercurial and prone to drama; the musicians vie to be one of the boys.

Music management and administration is an odd profession; it rarely starts out as an ambition in itself. It is something that people drift into; someone knows someone – or worse, wants to. The difficult recruits are those who come into the business as fans, full of opinions and preconceived ideas. They become stars by association; they are quick to become puffed up with an importance they have always coveted. Some managers become fussy nurse-maids; others are shadows humbling themselves ostentatiously before greatness; some are simply as venal as pimps. Some care too much, others not enough. In America, however, a new breed of manager has come up: young, musically trained, viewing classical music as just another business. It may make it all a lot less perfumed; it also makes for a briskness, a toughness, an ability to concentrate on the bottom line.

Larry Tucker, sharing the limousine out to the airport with Dennis, is a manager with Columbia Artists and a 33-year-old former pianist from Brooklyn and Forest Hills. His father, something in industrial plumbing supplies, just wanted him to get on in life. His mother wanted more than that. She sat by the piano ('endlessly for hours and hours') supervising the son's practice. He gave it up when he was 24. 'A little better than average technique and a lousy ear' is the way he sums up his talent now. At Columbia he manages Martha Argerich, Rudolf Firkusny, Maurizio Pollini and Alexis Weissenberg. It is hardly surprising that he has not touched the piano himself for years. He is slight, dark and earnest about his profession as befits one with a bachelor's degree in music from the University of Washington and a master's from Ann Arbor, Michigan.

Tucker talks of distance, of not letting his opinions get in the way and of integrity: 'It doesn't matter whether I feel an artist is good, bad, indifferent or great.' How different he is from his British counterpart who would somehow suggest that all he is really doing is looking after his friends: the cult of the amateur versus the professional. Does Larry Tucker earn even a tenth of the income of any of the major artists in his division? There is no way of telling from the anonymity of his wardrobe, the tidiness of his regular three-weekly haircut, the sense of significance with which he makes for the phone wherever he is. Yesterday he bade farewell to Daniel Barenboim and the Orchestre de Paris in Austin, Texas. Today he comes to greet the London Symphony Orchestra in Washington.

By American standards, there is not much commission to be made from the LSO tour for Columbia Artists. There is always the endless squabbling by telex over who pays for what: somewhere still is that unpaid limousine bill from last summer's trip to Chicago. At least eastern European orchestras will do without trimmings, will share rooms in squalid hotels, put up with having less and playing more – but in exchange the tour presenters have to pay their entire overseas travel costs. What an American management firm really likes is a nice, cheap, noisy, flamboyant Communist dance company to tour: low costs, full houses, big profits. But Columbia Artists and the LSO have done business together for years. The music world of concert engagements, recording contracts, débuts and opportunities is prone to such close relationships. When you come down to it, the classical music business is such a marginal event in the modern world that everyone in it is, perforce, on the same side.

Over a ginger ale in the British Airways VIP lounge at Dulles, Dennis and Larry go over the division of responsibilities yet again. To Dennis's ample care falls the orchestra, the buses and the Capitol Hilton. To Larry falls the delicate task of watching over Claudio Abbado, his health, patience and comfort, the limousine and the suite at the Watergate Hotel. To the players of the LSO, an American tour is an adventure, a lark. 'Getting away from the missus' is a well-known LSO catch phrase. To Claudio Abbado, this is serious music-making to which end he will devote himself entirely. He is bringing his own orchestra to the land where he is known best as principal guest conductor of the great Chicago Symphony. Comparisons are inevitable, so too is trouble. The desires of Abbado and the LSO cannot possibly coincide entirely during the next few days. Dennis and Larry down one last, long cold drink. The plane has landed; let the play begin.

Tuesday, arrival in Washington

Slowly, very slowly, the musicians trickle round a far corner into the customs hall. Sue Mallet clutching a gigantic red file ('my brains' as she calls it) rushes ahead first and falls upon Dennis as on a long-lost cousin. Her new perm is much admired and certain mishaps from last summer are fondly recalled before Dennis's box of pre-registered room keys is produced with a flourish. Sue swings into action: clearing a large patch on the customs hall floor she lays out the envelopes in alphabetical order totally ignoring the displeasure of a senior American immigration official. He is cowed by one glance from the iron eye of the Englishwoman on her knees beneath his ample stomach. One of the characteristics of the LSO (and, by definition, those who work for it) is that it has grown quite used to getting away with things, to pulling something out of the bag, to being regarded as delightfully bad. The carryings-on down on the customs hall floor is part of it: it is not an entirely grown-up way of behaving. Is it possible, for instance, to imagine the weighty and responsible Berlin Philharmonic scrabbling about the floor for room keys? As an orchestra lives, it might be said, so does it play.

What happens over those brown envelopes captures in an instant the particular character of the LSO: not a soul moves to offer any help, neither with the keys, nor with the baggage which Sue is busily trying to direct into the right heap at the same time. It is a matter of pride with her, mistaken some might say, that as long as she is around her chaps do not carry suitcases. Slowly, the musicians move into a semi-circle around her. They stand and wait. Over a hundred musicians flocking in at once after a seven-hour flight from London and it is up to Sue to place the names of them all. This is both some kind of test and of proof. She is, after all, their employee. The old LSO macho swagger exerts itself in one silent, defiant gaze. But, at the same time, they want her to remember, they want her to assuage their insecurity, to show that their name at least is remembered and, therefore, of consequence.

It is a bizarre and rather silly piece of ritual, but then so much is when a hundred grown men feel as though they are being herded facelessly together. It is the nub of the problem that besets every orchestra. The LSO solves it by adopting a swagger, by somehow revelling in its reputation for 'booze and

Tails, Moscow

birds'. Other richer, more secure ensembles solve it by adopting a heavy pomposity, a tendency to boast and to be smug. One by one, the brown envelopes disappear and the hall empties. 'They won't give a bloody inch, will they,' says Sue Mallet afterwards. It sounds almost like praise.

A few other clues obtrude: there is, for instance, the way that the orchestra's leader, Michael Davis, and the principal cellist, Douglas 'Duggie' Cummings, come through holding their instruments. These are the insignia of their office; of course they must carry them along while others leave them to the official movers. It is not that Davis's Vuillaume violin or Cummings's cello are intrinsically more valuable in themselves. Could the sheriff travel without his gun? Upon Mike and Duggie rests the responsibility of practising and being prepared, and upon them alone it would seem.

The orchestra has almost cleared customs before Larry Tucker from Columbia Artists comes into his own. Where another conductor might be first off the plane, Claudio Abbado creeps out at the very back of the rank and file. No special sense of charisma surrounds him. He is nearly 50, not as slender as he once was, and his fine black hair is greying at the sides. He is dressed – concealed rather – in drab, dark colours. Only the keenest eye would note the stylish cut and fabric. His eyes are creased and red: small slits set into a large dark shadow. Five *'Lohengrins'* at La Scala in Milan have wrung him out. Abbado is subtle, serious, introspective and consumed by some questing inner spirit. This is the principal conductor, within a few weeks to become music director, of the London Symphony Orchestra: an unlikely marriage. The limousine will take him to the privacy of the Watergate Hotel, attentive Larry at his side. Tomorrow morning he will work and study; tomorrow afternoon he and the orchestra will meet for a rehearsal.

On its first American tour in 1912, the LSO played 31 concerts in 21 days. So, as Sue Mallet rightly says, 'It's a doddle now really, isn't it?' Just as she is gathering up her red file to go out to the bus, a call draws her back. There unclaimed on the customs bench, with an old LSO touring label, is a large green suitcase. The one tag bears the name of Pashanko Dimitroff, the Bulgarian double bass player and LSO member who has not been able to play since his second leg was amputated a few years ago. Musicians are superstitious; so much of what they do, after all, is inexplicable. Pashanko's ghostly green suitcase is not a welcome omen.

Wednesday morning, Capitol Hilton

Early next morning in the irrepressibly cheery hotel coffee shop, the tables and counters are taken over by musicians trying to settle into life on tour. At home, 'the orchestra' as such hardly exists: musicians rush into sessions and out again, there is no time to catch up, no need to get to know anyone or anything that is not immediate. On tour, players come together, let off steam, share secrets and running jokes. 'Foxhole buddies' are made. Five weeks of

Kurt-Hans Goedicke, *Henry Wood Hall, London*

neglect: no bills, no children, no jingle sessions. The instruments are packed away at Kennedy Center and, for the most part, given no thought. This afternoon will be soon enough.

Over a spartan breakfast in one corner of the room, the pinched and polished face of Kurt-Hans Goedicke, timpanist, gazes into the distance. He has not the peace of mind to stroll out to the National Gallery or the Smithsonian. There is a four-hour rehearsal ahead and he will not rest easy until his drums are before his eyes, safe and sound. 'This set of kettles is the greatest I've ever played. They're from Ludwig of Chicago, fairly sloppily made so they won't last as long as the German ones the orchestra used to have (they took two men to lift and they'll last a hundred years). But these are irreplaceable; newer models than these don't have the same depth of sound and warmth. But you play them, you put the covers on and then it's up to the gods what happens to them. If the porters drop my timp, there's nothing I can do.'

He has been up for hours. His exercise cycle has been completed, his face has been creamed, his wardrobe laid out and forty pairs of Tonking cane timp sticks have been lovingly unfolded from his collection of hotel laundry bags. 'You have to pack them in plastic – cloth bags could cut half the life off the heads. They're made of felt from merino wool and so soft that the friction could rub them all the way down.' He has, perhaps, 200 sets of sticks, many made for him by other timp players in Germany. 'I know exactly what I want' – and he means *exactly*. As he sees it, there is often only one set of sticks out of his entire collection with which he can play a certain note. The famous B flat tremolo in Mahler's Fifth for instance: 'You must know there's a noise but if you can hear it, it's too loud. You sweat blood; one stick jumps up and it's murder. It's like shooting someone right between the eyes – it's there, or it's nothing. Pick a slender, hard, brutal sound . . . you've blown it. And half the bloody people in the orchestra I play for don't know the first thing about it.'

Every orchestra player hears music through the ears of his own instrument. Each instrumentalist believes that his contribution is unique. This tendency is even more exaggerated in a good timpanist: he plays alone, there is no other instrument that can even approximate his sound and besides he cannot, right at the back of an orchestra, even hear anyone else. A timpanist lives in this world of his own and yet he must exactly place every note not only where it is written but where it will fall in the natural cadence of an orchestra's phrasing and timing. Wrists like butter, an unerring sense of rhythm: in short, a good timpanist needs to be a fanatic, like Goedicke. To be a timpanist is to be more than usually misunderstood: and all orchestra musicians see themselves as that. In music there are legendary figures known to all: Stanley Drucker, clarinet, in New York; Myron Bloom, horn, in Paris; Ray Still, oboe, in Chicago. No one has ever called a timpanist 'legendary'. The instrument is the orchestra's pulse; no one listens to it, until it goes wrong.

Few of Goedicke's colleagues knew anything about his years' long fight with calfskin membranes, resolved only recently when he gave in and went over to plastic. Who but a timpanist would understand the sensitivity of the organic material, the problems of placing a note on pores that would be larger where brown hair once grew than black hair? The Royal Festival Hall finally defeated him: he would tune at 7.45, check and double check (as is his way) and come out for an 8 o'clock concert to find a G instead of an A. The air conditioning had done it again. 'With a plastic head it's a devil of a job to get to the right sound but once you have, the intonation is as pure as driven snow.' Not surprisingly, if there is one thing guaranteed to rile Goedicke, it is a conductor telling him how to play. 'Abbado used to ask me to use harder sticks so finally I went to him and said, "You tell me what sound you want and I'll decide how to get that effect." He wanted a more percussive, less voluminous sound, he said. Fine. Now he has it. Harder sticks had nothing to do with it. Conductors do not understand either.'

He is the outsider, playing alone. He never plays percussion and even when there is a second timpani part, he holds himself away somehow from the other player. Seated behind his kettles, rummaging constantly in his plastic laundry bags for another set of sticks, tuning and adjusting constantly, he dwells in his own land: a perfectionist and a loner. He sees himself that way. He will describe himself as the orchestra's only foreigner (born and brought up in Berlin). It is untrue because like most orchestras the LSO has its refugees, but it feels true to him. He was 10 when World War II ended. His brother had been in the Hitler Youth and later became a bomber and fighter pilot; his father was in the war-effort chemical industry; their street was absorbed into the Russian sector. It is not a childhood he much wants to remember let alone discuss with his LSO colleagues. He knows too that they laugh at him: at his creams, colognes, velvet-collared tails and neat black handbag. They may laugh but their vote put him on the board of directors; he was vice-chairman of the orchestra. Like the music it plays, the dynamics of an orchestra are always more complicated than they seem.

Wednesday afternoon rehearsal, Kennedy Center

The Kennedy Center has been open for ten years. There is something quaintly old-fashioned about its concert hall: perhaps it is the rich mixture of red carpet, swagged drapes, gold lettering and great vistas of pale marble slabs. It suggests a safe, slightly anonymous but stuffy formality – perfect for Washington, a one-company town, as it were, given over to politics and power and all the conservative trappings of doing well in the world. Supporting the arts is part of those trappings.

Washington is the ideal place for the LSO to start its American tour. The hall will be full, the highly respected *Washington Post* will doubtless sends its senior music critic, there will be a satisfactory sprinkling of black ties. The concert will have all the hallmarks of a prestigious occasion and actually not matter too much. It would be a mistake for the LSO to come too soon to New York. Jet lag, tension, nerves, unease: who knows what might go wrong? In New York, reputations are made; in Washington, they are confirmed. A good reception here is important psychologically – it always helps to have done well. It is enough as it happens, because the LSO will forgive Abbado anything if a concert goes well. He will need that forgiveness. He has been principal conductor of the LSO since 1979: rehearsals have always been the one area of incompatibility between them. He believes in careful preparation, working on detail, getting things right. The LSO enjoys spontaneity, pulling it all together at the last moment, their famous 'smash-and-grab raids'.

This afternoon's rehearsal has been called for two. In the lobby of the Capitol Hilton, musicians slowly come together in small groups. In the hotel shop there is a brisk trade in leisure and sports magazines: stocking up for the long hours ahead on stage. The orchestra has not seen Abbado for a few weeks; but they have not forgotten. A stir over by the elevators: Anthony Camden, 'the Whizzer', principal oboe, LSO chairman, appears touting an impressive red leather briefcase and a dashing tan. Mysterious property business in Florida all last week delayed his arrival; at least he is here now.

Camden is, in many ways, the central source of energy in the orchestra. He is the most forceful chairman so far in a history of characters. He has the distinction of having had more adjectives applied to him than almost any comparable figure in London's musical world: brilliant, mercurial, hard-headed, extraordinary, devious, slippery. He has been called everything in his time and cheerfully disregards most of it. If he is talked about that much, he reckons, the LSO must be doing something right. 'Brilliant' certainly fits: he has the imagination and ingenuity of a fine oboist but he also understands this orchestra in his bones and fights for it like a tough and wily fox. Other London orchestra men at least pay lip service to wishing their competitors well. Camden simply never mentions any but the LSO. It is as if others do not exist. That he is not just a bright young man on the make is due to a side of him that outsiders often overlook: when he sits in the orchestra it is not as Mr Chairman but as first oboe. It is the most exposed of positions; the oboe is at the very core of an orchestra, its soul at its most plaintive and honest. The wrong kind of tension, a meanness of attack and all beauty will be lost. Camden is in the top handful of oboists in the world. The conjuring tricks by which he controls the LSO and keeps it running, must not come too close to that musical centre within.

As always he has turned up just in time: how, when and where from is anyone's guess. Apart from anything else Anthony Camden is the only one who can really deal with Abbado. It works both ways, perhaps; Claudio asks for artistry and so with him there can be no pretence. No sleight of hand can save a phrase on the oboe. The musical asset-stripper from Totteridge and the Italian son of Parsifal from Milan: they are one of music's odd couples.

Anthony Camden, *London*

Audition in the Henry Wood Hall, London. Martin Gatt with a student, Nicholas Hunka and Roy Jowitt

(Music is full of these partnerships: the acknowledged saintly one and his worldy alter ego: Vladimir Horowitz and Wanda Toscanini, Yehudi and Diana Menuhin, Igor Stravinsky and Robert Craft.)

In truth, they have more in common than meets the eye. They are both part of a musical aristocracy; they have grown up in this stellar world and have always belonged to it. Camden's father was the great bassoonist, Archie Camden, one of the legends of English wind playing. Abbado grew up in Milan, part of a milieu that embraced La Scala, Toscanini and the Verdi Conservatory, of which his brother is now director. They share a charm that is both immediate and somehow unreachable. They are inherently elusive, belonging, for all their allegiances, only to themselves. Sometimes it is like having two magical Peter Pans at the head of an orchestra, one temporal, one spiritual. More everyday folk might find this exasperating but musicians have often a wayward streak. (Even stolid, respectable Brahms liked to go out jumping in the grass.) So if Abbado wants to programme a piece that is enormously expensive to mount and Camden chooses to encourage him, it does have its quid pro quo. Abbado's presence on this long tour, is an example. His wife, Gabriella, and son, Sebastian, are at home in London: travelling around the world with the LSO makes no sense except as an act of loyalty. Camden has always fostered the belief that the LSO *needs* Abbado for its very artistic survival. ('Commercial work is doughnuts and jam,' Camden has always said, 'Claudio is our protein.')

It is 1.50. With the ease of a man with hours to spare, Camden slides around a lobby pillar having a few moments here and there with his constituents. He manages to catch the eye of all who want 'just a few minutes' with him, and they are many. His charm is hard at work; he is warm, utterly disarming, enthusiastic, a superb operator. It is not a talent usually given to musicians. Camden is one of the orchestra's strengths and also its weaknesses. As Chairman, he runs the LSO.

None of this makes life any easier for the unfortunate man waiting on the other side of the lobby wearing his perpetual LSO look of exasperation: Peter Hemmings is the LSO's managing director. The buses leave for rehearsal any second and half of his orchestra are not even in sight. The chaos, the instinctive disregard for order, comes hard to a man prepared for life by Mill Hill School, Gonville and Caius College, Cambridge (an upper second) and national service as a 2nd lieutenant with the Royal Corps of Signals.

In his grey flannel suit, Hemmings looks like the managing director. It sets him apart from the orchestra – which is, of course, both his employer and his work force – in just the way that Camden's natty sports outfit does not. Hemmings, as he is the first to admit, is running the LSO by an unfortunate career accident. He is really an opera man: he had a marvellous stint setting up the Scottish National Opera Company before being invited to Australia to run the Sydney Opera House. That he was the seventh general manager in thirteen years might have tipped him off before he moved there with wife, Jane, and five children. Joan Sutherland and her husband, Richard Bonynge, are Australia's Mr and Mrs Opera; it was perhaps naïve really to imagine that they would see themselves as answerable to him. 'A terrible setback for me – it banged me down with a vengeance,' he says matter-of-factly. At least when Anthony Camden called him in Sydney (characteristically, it was at three in the morning) to join the LSO, he was an older, wiser man.

To be the managing director of the LSO has all the security of marriage to Henry VIII. Only a fool would imagine otherwise. Hemmings is not a fool; he is a decent headmasterly type with a good heart trying to do an impossible job: 'If you're too successful', he says with a very small smile, 'you can jeopardize your position here just as easily as if you're unsuccessful.' A self-governing body, busy with making music, needs someone to run things well. But if he runs them too well, they will fire him for encroaching on their territory: the spirit of democracy is keenly guarded.

The buses outside start their engines. Hemmings takes off his glasses, puts away his lists and notes, and goes out trusting yet again that all will be well: and trying to believe it as brave officers do. It is only because of his tireless fund-raising efforts that this tour is taking place: it was not definite until January, three years after it was first mooted, at the very last second in musical time. He looks around for a friendly face politely inviting him to sit down – some habits die hard. Every man for himself here. At least he fares better than Sue Mallet who cannot find a seat and stands all the way. The thorny problem of being moved around has, for years, encapsulated the whole management–player confrontation in American orchestras. If there is one thing humiliating to a man (probably a distinguished professor of music at some august academy), it is having his head counted, his name ticked off on a list like an errant minor. American musicians always point to the bus of the London orchestra as a symbol of the great achievement of self-government. No lists, no counting, no names, no overseeing 'prefects'. It is assumed that any orchestra grown up enough to run itself is grown up enough to get on a bus – no matter how it behaves once it is on.

Claudio Abbado sits very patiently in his dressing room backstage at the Kennedy Center waiting for the rehearsal. He has with him a baton case and a miniature score. How frugal he seems compared to other conductors who always fill the spaces in which they find themselves: a *Tristan* for '87, a world première next month, a wad of telephone messages and letters, music and memos cast everywhere. For the concert, Abbado will not even have the score. He conducts from memory; the printed page is a distraction, he says, a barrier between himself and the musicians. By knowing a piece that well, he feels that he can more quickly fix something if it goes wrong – a trumpet comes in four bars early, a bassoon takes a repeat while the rest of the orchestra plays on. He has done his work; no last minute cramming now. Besides, he is tired and his eyes are sore. The faithful Larry Tucker will have to find an optician; Claudio's contact lenses are dirty and he does not know how to clean them.

He smiles apologetically at such helplessness. Abbado has a very sweet smile but it rarely just appears; it has to creep over his face, making its way by stealth. He is at his best, his most direct on the podium during a concert. Even friends sometimes say that the rest of the time he sleepwalks, that he has been consumed by music as if by the religious spirit. That may be; what is sure is that when he is old, he will be revered just as those old, distinguished musicians to whom he himself is so drawn: Artur Rubinstein when he was alive ('How I would love to be like him – he is so young in his heart,' he once said) or Rudolf Serkin ('Serkin said to me, "Claudio, before I die I would like to play all the Mozart concertos with you." Imagine that this great man said that to me.') Klemperer, Matačić, Stokowski, Celibidache, Böhm, Casals: music has always adored its ageing gods. All that is asked is that they stand there and be very old and great, monuments to survival. One day, Abbado will surely make a spectacular old conductor.

For the moment he has a problem with the expectations of those who confuse his charm with warmth. He is one of music's magical children: he loves to conduct the LSO, and he loves many of its musicians. He does not understand that other manifestations are wanted from him. Here in Washington, they would understand. They call it 'pressing the flesh'. So there are small hurts and disappointments: if Claudio knew, he would doubtless put them right. He is a kind man, but distant. 'I hadn't seen Claudio for weeks', says Michael Davis, LSO's leader. 'I got on the plane yesterday. I said, "Claudio, great, how's Gabriella? How's Sebastian?" He said, "fine". That's it. No "How's Sue? How's Ben?" It's silly but it hurts.'

Abbado is the product of old and complicated cultures: part Arab, Jew, Sicilian, Norman. Within him there runs a strangely Victorian streak; controlled or repressed rather than cold. This afternoon he will be rehearsing Mahler's First Symphony. Of course he is a marvellous interpreter of Mahler: so many aspects of the composer's character bear similarities to his own. Mahler's music with its seething undercurrents, occasionally catching fire with an almost white heat, can in an instant drop from the loudest rasping note to the softest whisper: just as Abbado can cut himself off the second a piece is over. A last passionate chord and Claudio's face masks over as he automatically glances down to check his waistcoat studs.

A polite Mahler performance would be meaningless. Some of his climaxes are slightly diseased, as if a boil were bursting. There is vulgarity, coarseness but also moments of unearthly beauty. Beneath the barrage of sound, the constant holding back and building up, Abbado's own release is both inevitable and in the service of the music. He gives of himself totally: to the music, if

Michael Davis, *Leningrad*

not to the audience. There are conductors who find it easier to 'let go' – Leonard Bernstein being their apotheosis – but Abbado neither can nor wants to escape his natural restraint and concealed fervour. Abbado hugs his passion to himself; he, at least, never doubts that it is there.

Time to walk out. Remembering Yuri Simonov's assertive bustle, it is interesting to see Abbado merely cover the distance from sidestage to podium. His walk is all business; it is the walk of a small shopkeeper going to check his stock. A few smiles that confirm his pleasure at being with old friends, that is all. No jokes, no speeches: just the downbeat after a quick glance to be sure that the right faces are in place. They call this 'a real Claudio piece'. It is a real LSO piece too. Beethoven, Schubert, Schumann wrote of the uplifting spirit of mankind; all of life is in Mahler, including the seedy parts. The First Symphony is very much a work of many instruments playing together; there are few spots with a delicate chamber music feeling. So if the LSO is taking time to settle down, is slow to match Abbado's precision, or is even plagued with hangovers – any hint of sloppiness will not be as evident. At the beginning of this rehearsal, only the strengths show.

The opening bars of the first movement suggest the awakening of nature. The strings play long-held harmonics, an eerie white noise like a ringing in the ears. Some orchestras might sound too rich, others too thin and shaky: this one produces exactly the right intensity. Two horns play in thirds, a beautiful, singing solo. No British horn player has ever been able to move beyond the shadow of the great Denis Brain but David Cripps, the LSO principal, has a clear floating tone with corners that are always neat. Every orchestra has its 'stars' and they may be found on many instruments. Even an ear that could not recognize the special quality of their sound, however, could quickly spot in rehearsal who they were: 'stars' sit with more assurance. If there is a drawn-out scene with a conductor they will often pay no attention: not out of sullenness but from the assumption that it could not have anything to do with them and that, besides, they have some bit of business to do with their instrument or music that takes precedence. David Cripps, dark-haired, red-cheeked, all quiet and unassuming innocence, sees himself as such a star. When Cripps went on a scholarship to the Royal Academy of Music, his professor was Jim Brown who sits by him now as assistant principal. That is one reason why musicians are colleagues from the start: talent knows no hierarchy of age or experience.

And then the trouble starts. Three trumpets go offstage to play a solo marked 'from a distance'. Mahler, a great conductor himself, left nothing to chance in his orchestration. He marks clearly in the score that they are to return at number 3, a quiet moment as it happens. Abbado has decided that only a nitwit would disturb such a soft phrase and that they must come back at number 9, a thunderous forte. Naturally, they wander back whenever the mood takes them. Abbado never raises his voice. He always allows the other man time to make his point however irrelevant. If he were judged only by how he runs rehearsals and how he deals with such a confrontation, he would seem to be too ineffectual to be a conductor. He has no desire to impose discipline; he sees it as a violation of man's democratic spirit. (Abbado to the brass: 'You're playing too loud.' First trumpet: 'You're wrong. You can't hear properly from where you are.' Claudio: 'Are you telling me about balance?' Trumpet: 'Yes'.)

He will neither assert his will once and for all nor let a matter drop. He allows himself to be drawn into discussions that he cannot win just by dint of having allowed them to happen in the first place. Another lesser man would reel beneath the incessant blows to his pride and ego. Not Claudio: he is like a devout priest unable to hit back, welcoming punishment as proof of his faith and as an example to others. It is a hopelessly impractical role to play in front of the brazen LSO. He has been like this with them for years, which is why the trumpets dare now to stare him down. 'How do we know where is number 9?' they ask, all innocence, as if they could not hear it once and remember. 'It's not marked in our parts.'

What follows is even more unfortunate. Abbado turns to Michael Davis, the leader and nominal head of the orchestra, and puts the problem into his hands. 'You take care of it,' he says as if discipline were beneath artistic consideration. Michael Davis, first-rate fiddler as he is, has if anything less authority over the LSO than Abbado. The last thing he wants is trouble. ('You can't give them a bollocking can you? It can't be a war, not if a leader's ever going to be successful, can it?') Now there are two of them made to look silly. Meanwhile, a couple of minor actors, wind players both, use this diversion to pop out. Naturally, it is incumbent upon Abbado either not to notice or to pretend that they have gone in search of a men's room not a quick smoke. They come back together a few, sad notes too late for their entry. Just another Abbado rehearsal.

He bores the players; he rarely lets them play on to the natural end of a phrase. He stops and starts, a disaster with most orchestras, but especially one as energetic as this. He sings too little, he talks too much, his comments are flat and businesslike. And yet, in some inexplicable way, he binds the orchestra to him. On one level, the players kick against him, complain and defy him. A popular LSO saying these days goes: 'We rehearse because Claudio needs to practise his memory.' And yet, deep down, he must reach them because when the concert comes, most of the details he has worried over have been fixed. That does not happen spontaneously.

A great musician is one who comes to some old warhorse for the thousandth time and is still discovering it. The LSO has played Mahler again and again for Abbado. They rely on him to approach each performance as if it were the first. If he were as callous towards the music as they profess to be, they would fire him. He is here only because they believe in him. Tomorrow night for 52 minutes of Mahler One, he will give them his all: with every gesture and glance, every caressing movement of his hands, every naked plea in his eyes, he will share with them all his inner feeling and thought. But in the middle of a long rehearsal with another still to come, tomorrow night seems a long, long way off.

It is dusk in Washington. Sue Mallet is still scurrying about, 'trying to make life easier for the lads', as she calls it. This time it is one last phone call to the Hollinger Box Company in Arlington, Virginia, trying to wheedle delivery of twelve cardboard hanging boxes to carry the orchestra's tails around America. Most of them are still in baskets at Kennedy Center, crumpled and smelly from the last concerts in London. Heifetz used to lose 1½ pounds every time he performed and he didn't play the whole concert (it was 3 pounds if he did). Peter Hemmings does not react well to the casual observation that London's Philharmonia Orchestra at least looks as if it has heard the words 'dry cleaning'. It is an unknowingly cutting comparison. The Philharmonia's urbane manager, Christopher Bishop, and Hemmings were organ scholars together at Cambridge. Bishop certainly runs the most elegant and 'European' of the London orchestras at the moment – even if Hemmings has the busiest.

Imagine the Festival Hall bar just before a concert: if the Philharmonia is on tonight it has the select atmosphere of a good golf club: straight backs, well-cut hair, laundered shirts, pressed clothes. When the LSO is on, it is as if a rugby club is holding its annual general meeting. Hemmings considers the matter of the LSO concert wardrobe and loyally fights against anything that could be construed as criticism. Finally, he gives in: 'It's horrid, isn't it. It's very difficult to know what to do about it. They're all self-employed and as long as you don't get too close, I suppose it's all right.'

Sue's lads are currently scattered across Washington. Some thrifty, dependable souls are eating together at cheap burger bars. A few are milling around the hotel in a lonely sort of way. Every orchestra has its wallflowers; those who, on tour, always end up parked in lobby armchairs wistfully watching their colleagues who have an easier, lighter touch. The flock of nameless beauties that settled around the Kennedy Center stage door during the rehearsal have all been claimed. 'I don't know and I don't ask,' says Sue Mallet firmly. 'As far as I'm concerned they could all be absolutely anybody's sister.'

On the other side of town, Claudio Abbado is sitting in his Watergate suite, studying scores, ordering room service. And at about this time, Michael Davis, LSO leader, puts down the phone after his second call of the day home to North London and wonders how he will get through the next five weeks. 'I'm so bloody homesick, I can't bear it. I woke up last night and I just missed my wife and kids. I want to go home. That's all.' He goes down to the bar for a quick drink to cheer himself up. 'Hello', growls Bob Bourton, principal bassoon and board member. Couldn't miss you in rehearsal with the lights on that shiny bald head of yours.' It is a silly crack; it has been made before and will again because each time he hears it, Davis smarts.

The man who sat in his chair before him would never have made that mistake. John Georgiadis was one of those huge, hungry characters full of imagination and daring about whom tales will be told years after he has ceased to play. Until he soured, before his exploits as orchestra leader and ringleader palled even on him, he was a marvellous violinist. He played with strength and musicality; his section were 'his guys'; he talked to them that way and yet with one fiery look could silence them. 'Me Tarzan, you Jane' is an exciting way to lead an orchestra. It also lends itself to going over the top, a condition to which musicians, volatile as they are, are prone. During Georgiadis's last years as leader of the LSO he seemed to appoint himself the conscience of the conducting world: Celibidache, the ageing eccentric, became his guru, others were his whipping post. When the first violin section began to acquire an international reputation as a graveyard (of music as well as conductors), he decided that he had had enough. Michael Davis was invited in for a bit of conscientious spring cleaning.

In orchestra life, the man who is gone is always the one who is best loved. Hear the way they talk now of André Previn, their last principal conductor. Every visit he makes to the LSO is a reaffirmation of how dearly he is missed – his jokes, his easy-going ways, his professionalism. Now that he is committed to the Royal Philharmonic Orchestra and, of course, now that the LSO feels confident of Abbado. Every orchestra is alike. Eugene Ormandy was music director of the Philadelphia Orchestra for forty-two years: and still, at the very end of his tenure, there were those who pined for the golden days of Stokowski.

Music is the one art in which it is death to feel too strongly another man's shadow. It is the only art form almost wholly preoccupied with the act of re-creation, again and again. There is always some musician somewhere who has played, or is playing, it better. Should Isaac Stern play the Beethoven violin concerto with the sound of Kreisler in his ears? Should Abbado approach Beethoven thinking of Bruno Walter? There must be faith in the validity of each person's performance.

Michael Davis, at this point, probably remembers Georgiadis more clearly, more frequently than those who sat behind him. Or perhaps the man's shadow is just an excuse. Davis is also homesick for the North of England. He grew up until he was 35 with the Hallé Orchestra, the band of Barbirolli, Manchester's own band, run by local worthies, a well-behaved, well-tempered part of the city's life. Mike was part of a community; he had always lived there. His violinist father was in the Hallé when he was a boy and still was when Davis became co-principal at the age of 23. People in Manchester knew who Eric Davis and his son Mike were. Who in the Greater London area thinks of the London Symphony Orchestra as his own? Once an orchestra belonged to one man's royal court; now Davis is coming to grips with the ultimate development of not belonging to anyone at all.

'You know what I think it is in the end? You go and play in places like Bradford and Sheffield and you feel you're playing to the same people every week. You're part of their lives and they're part of yours. Very shortly after I became leader of the LSO, we went to Manchester on tour. I walked out on stage at the Free Trade Hall, which I'd done for hundreds of concerts with the Hallé but this time it was like meeting a solid wall of sound. I was the local lad who was now leading the ultra-glamorous LSO. I belonged and I'd made it into the big time. The silly part is that for me leading the Hallé always was the big time.'

Of course it was; his father played in it for 33 years. It was he unusually, who taught Michael the violin – he was 4½ when he started lessons, 18 when they stopped. From the age of 8, Mike was taken in regularly to play for Sir John Barbirolli. In a community, a conductor has the chance to nurture talent for his own orchestra. Anthony Camden's father, for instance, was sent to the Royal Northern College on a personal scholarship from the Hallé's music chief. The conductor wanted a bassoonist trained in a certain German way for his orchestra. In the old days when a conductor stayed most of the year, many years of his life with an orchestra and could invite whom he chose to play for it, he could make that investment for the future. And thus Barbirolli watched over Mike's development: it was he who arranged for him to study with Hugh Bean, then leader of the Philharmonia, at the Royal College in London; he who arranged a scholarship from the Countess of Munster Trust so that Davis could study with Henrik Szeryng in Paris. And when the studying and polishing was finished, he did not launch his protégé into the solo field – it was neither what Mike wanted nor what he had been groomed for. He brought him back to the Hallé.

'Barbirolli had all the qualities everybody knows about. He was the kind of person who could make an ordinary person into a good player and a good one great. It's easy to stand in front of a good band and look good. The difficult bit for me is to stand in front of a not-so-good one and make them better. Some people in that orchestra would have walked through fire and water for the little sod and my Dad was one of them. When Barbirolli was there the Hallé was a lot like the LSO: it was very warm, there were a lot of characters in it, a lot of knock-about humour, they played with a lot of balls. If you grow up with an orchestra like that, you're bound to have a strange, magical feeling for it. It's sad though because there was a kind of hang-up in Manchester that however proud you were, however determined, there was a sneaking feeling in the back of your mind that you had to come and do it in the big smoke. And now I've done it – and I want to go home.'

At the Barbican, London. Henry Greenwood, Claudio Abbado, Kurt-Hans Goedicke, James Judd and Edward Downes (*The three conductors who conducted Stockhausen's* Brücken *in 1983*)

It is not so easy and he probably does not mean that in its literal sense. To be a first-rate leader of an orchestra is in itself a separate profession. Traditionally, leaders neither want to become soloists, nor do they. Life for them is better as it is. There are glorious solos to play within the orchestra and chances to play concertos and chamber music as a guest elsewhere. There is the satisfaction of being a leader among men and having the massive orchestra repertoire to work on. It is the best of all worlds. Joseph Silverstein, for instance, concertmaster or leader of the Boston Symphony Orchestra for nearly 30 years, is more famous in America as a result of the BSO's countless television appearances than Henrik Szeryng, himself among the more sought-after of soloists. Even in the major American orchestras, where string sections are full of frustrated soloists, one-time music school 'hot shots', angry and bitter at finding themselves in an orchestra at all, the concertmaster is always one musician pretty much at peace with his station in life. Until, that is, he gets bitten by the conducting bug: Silverstein has become music director of the Utah Symphony in Salt Lake City, which even at its highest, can never match the musical inspiration of Boston.

Once having led the London Symphony Orchestra, it is not easy to move. London – with Vienna, Paris, Munich, Berlin, Amsterdam – is one of the major European capitals of the music world. However such a list differs, it never includes Manchester. How could Mike go back even were the job open? It is easy to say that it is the music that matters, but it is a wise and rare musician who can put that into practice. Glitter and the rewards of success have always been attractive. No British leader will quickly forget how Rodney Friend allowed himself to be wooed from the London Philharmonic to lead the New York Philharmonic. He soon returned. Today he leads the BBC Symphony Orchestra, a nine to five Maida Vale studio existence that could not be further from the fabled life of the New World. It was an interesting lesson in priorities.

So Michael Davis sits here in the Capitol Hilton, rubbing his hurts away. No dressing room for him today at the Kennedy Center: he moved in with Abbado. (This is actually better: 'You get a lot of nuts and bolts done while you're changing your trousers.') No invitation yet to the English Supper tomorrow night under the patronage of the British Ambassador and Lady Wright in honour of the London Symphony Orchestra. ('It bloody hurts having to wait around to see whether the LSO board is going to deign to include me.')

No hush when he calls for it in rehearsal, no reserved seat on the plane or bus, no honour and no respect: that is how it looks to him in the black, tired moments. 'I'm just one of eighty shareholders, and although as leader I can make my feelings and beliefs known just like anyone else can, that's the limit.'

And at the same time, Michael Davis is loving every minute of it. He has never felt so alive. The one fear common to all musicians is of reaching within and finding no reserves of misery, pain, resentment or anger. From where then would come the inspiration?

Thursday morning

The social aspects of the orchestra's appearance in Washington seem to be assuming an importance at least equal to the music. The supper party to be held in the marble halls of the British Embassy Residence should not be overlooked as an extension of the concert itself. Playing well is not enough; it must be seen to be a ritual event. One of the avenues available to an orchestra in its efforts to raise money is cultivating an image of culture chic. This happens neither by accident nor by sublime association. To be frank, the LSO is not gifted at working the rich. It seems to think that they are much like anyone else. Little by little, they are learning the ropes. Anthony Camden has picked up just the right note of young, eager, devoted musician in his speeches to businessmen. Peter Hemmings has been sent forth to companies for some straight managing director-to-managing director talk. The LSO is making friends with corporate life.

An executive who appreciates music can also appreciate the simple fact that this orchestra is the hardest-working in the world: '615 three-hour sessions last year' is coming to sound like Peter Hemmings' mantra.

What the LSO does not yet understand are the private rich. How could it with its own rough-and-ready anti-star personality? Any fashionable West End hairdresser or boutique owner could tell the LSO where it goes wrong. The wealthy need to be wooed, need to be made to feel that it is they who are special not the cheques that they sign. It requires patient understanding and natural respect for those who are stars in other fields. Captains of industry (retd) or philanthropic heiresses are not to be treated with the breezy familiarity accorded another LSO member. But running around and making a fuss of people is not the LSO way – even Abbado is often left to his own devices. 'Claudio's perfectly happy to look after himself,' says Sue Mallet. It explains why there is not even a cold drinks tray in his dressing room. What nannying there is to spare always goes to the lads. So to be a patron of the LSO requires dogged devotion.

All of which explains why a large, warm-hearted Yorkshireman in his sixties is still sitting around in his pyjamas and dressing gown late into the morning. He is fretting over the miserable collection of concert tickets on the table before him. Sir Jack Lyons is one of the LSO's largest private donors (Jack Maxwell is another). Perhaps he has himself given £100,000 in his time; it is nice that he prefers not to say. In his London kitchen over late night snacks, he and Edward Heath, another long-time friend, have plotted and planned how to win over influential supporters for the orchestra. It was in Sir Jack's drawing room that the man from Lloyd's was prevailed upon to look kindly upon the LSO's present finances, to take the long view concerning that quarter of a million pound plus overdraft. This Thursday evening concert at the Kennedy Center is sponsored by Sir Jack together with some of his good friends at Minet Insurance. He has flown to Washington specially. He brushes aside this support as 'just putting a bit of thrust in'. He is sponsoring one of the LSO concerts in New York too, even though he disapproves totally of it. ('What good can it possibly do them?') In short, Sir Jack Lyons has been generous to the LSO.

His support for music has a long history: the Yorkshire Symphony Orchestra, the Leeds Festival, the Royal Academy of Music and, for fifteen years, the LSO. He puts it all down to his wife who was an opera singer when they married thirty-nine years ago but it must also be in memory of himself as a small boy, the only one of six children not to be allowed music lessons and probably the only one who really longed for them. 'I wanted to learn the violin so much but my father was hard commercially, he didn't want to throw money down the drain. He said: "I'm sorry but I've wasted enough on the others."' To this day, he remembers his first record: it was Schubert's Serenade and he wore it out. So if he really can help the LSO, he cannot help but be proud of it. It shows most in his endearing attempt not to boast: 'Having had a reasonably successful commercial career, I am happy to have an involvement and to be doing good.' Actually, for a patron he is a model of delicacy. Many is the businessman who has given far less and soon started to talk proprietorially of 'my orchestra' or, worse, 'my band' and the concerts 'we' are playing.

As chairman of the LSO Trust – supposedly in charge of managing such a trust, in fact trying to keep it afloat – he knows only too well the scope of the LSO's resources. Here in America, it is hard to avoid comparisons. From Washington, for instance, the LSO goes to Boston and Philadelphia. The Boston Symphony Orchestra has an endowment behind it of $25 million. It has a budget of $20 million this year, it earns $16.5 million and the $3.5 million deficit is covered by a special fund-raising drive. The orchestra owns outright the historical Symphony Hall in which it plays. The Philadelphia Orchestra which, as the product of a financially conservative community, runs on a much smaller budget, is still spending $10.5 million this year. It has an endowment behind it of nearly $18 million and, to all intents and purposes, also owns its concert hall, the Academy of Music. Against such funding and such safety cushions, the LSO lives on a pittance and yet, its very survival depends on guarding its reputation as a top, world-class orchestra. It would appeal to a down-to-earth Yorkshireman like Sir Jack: in his own way, he enjoys a good fight and respects a good fighter.

The matter of his tickets, though, is one small fight that he will not win. Months ago, he ordered 36 of them through the LSO office – he was to pay for them all. Here they are, in twos and threes, dotted around various of the less desirable stretches of the Kennedy Center. The grand circle is barred to him. He has two 'excellent prospects' as LSO donors flying in for tonight's affair in their private plane. How can such people be shuffled off downstairs? Here at last the amazing Sue Mallet shows that even she has her weak point: Sir Jack Lyons's tickets are driving her dotty. As far as she is concerned, tickets are the worst things that ever happened to her or to an orchestra and she cannot imagine why he is carrying on.

Worse is to come in Boston where the little group of sponsors from the First National Bank of Boston are given seats way back, right on the edge, in different rows. Row U, seats 1 and 2 are by no stretch of the imagination VIP in Symphony Hall terms. 'In a hall with acoustics like this one', says Peter Hemmings crossly, 'it doesn't matter where you sit.' As if hearing properly had anything to do with it. Queries about such matters have a way of riling Peter Hemmings: 'I don't like mischievous talk' – any more than he likes the suggestion that Sir Jack is angry about this Washington nonsense, although exasperated might be the better word. After fifteen years, their old friend knows them well. 'I mean I don't give a darn about myself,' he says, 'they can kick me in the backside any time. But a sponsor or would-be sponsor, you want to give them a bit of special treatment, that's all.'

An hour before the concert, champagne flows in Sir Jack Lyons's apartment. A uniformed maid circulates with the canapés. Lady Lyons, majestically presented in shocking pink, jewellery and make-up, watches over the guests and talks of the London Symphony Orchestra with unblighted warmth and admiration. The Lyonses are doing their bit.

4: A Call to Arms

Friday morning, Boston, Mass.

On the flight to Boston this Friday morning, the orchestra is curiously quiet. A good concert is a release; its effects are immediate. It is physically so much easier to play an instrument when there is confidence: muscles loosen, breathing relaxes, the imperceptible responses of the body record the change. When it goes well, there is a feeling of being able to do anything. The hardest passages seem to play themselves, the instrument has suddenly been transformed from a defiant challenger to a trusted friend. Last night's concert in Washington should have produced exactly this sense of well-being: the Kennedy Center was full, the reception was marvellous, many 'bravos' from a standing house and on stage it felt right. 'Glorious Londoners' was the heading to the *Washington Post*'s review this morning. The well-being always fades too soon, but not usually this soon. As the LSO moves on to Boston, there is a prickly tension.

There are four cities in America where a visiting orchestra is on its mettle: New York (mostly because of the powerful critics of the *New York Times*), Boston, Chicago and Philadelphia – these last three because of the special nature of their own orchestras. To Europeans, Boston is perhaps the most unnerving because of Symphony Hall, a physical embodiment of tradition and musical superiority infinitely more European than American. Only the Musikverein in Vienna and the Concertgebouw in Amsterdam can match its reputation. Against all fashionable inclination to refurbish and glamorize, Symphony Hall still has its old black leather and wooden seats, its strips of tatty industrial carpet going up the aisles and its gloomy illumination. It is the epitome of old, moneyed, patrician Boston. The best have performed here; it is as if only their ghosts remain. That must explain the tension in the air.

Occasions like this put an extra pressure on an orchestra's special stars. They are the manifestation of its best self. It is to them that the others look to be moved, to be led musically. Often their solos are only five or six notes long, not necessarily played alone, and yet in these small phrases there is enough scope for imagination and beauty of sound to add a whole extra dimension to an orchestra. Its reputation will depend on how many of these particular voices it has, how many of these musicians who can do more than play the notes well. A conductor can impose his musical will only so far; there is an inevitable point when another man's imagination must take over.

Roy Jowitt and Claudio Abbado, *Carnegie Hall, New York*

In the concert hall, it is usually the great, vivid clashing tuttis that have the immediate effect. Later, it is as often the memory of the quiet, solitary phrases that linger. In music, as in all Western art, it is the individual voice that gives meaning to the whole. No matter if an audience cannot consciously notice the difference; those sitting around such a player will hear it and be affected. The men in the back, the rank and file, those who may never be heard alone for the rest of their careers, can nevertheless be inspired by such a colleague to give more, to sing out. It is this that makes an orchestra great: that it can draw inspiration not only from without but also from within. To be otherwise is to be without a substantial musical centre.

The LSO, of course, in its low-key way, does not make much ado about anyone's breathtaking phrases. What goes on in the passion of the moment out there is not alluded to in the camaraderie of the bus. But even a newcomer would surely single out as special two of the figures milling around on the journey to Boston. John Fletcher, tuba, and Maurice Murphy, principal trumpet, are a study in contrasts. Fletcher with his austerely etched face and biblical beard, storms away at the bottom of the brass section with a huge, Old Testament wrath. He pins down the entire orchestra with his great and growling tone. He pushes aside impatiently any suggestion of being an LSO star: he would rather be its conscience, and that too is part of his musical character. Every orchestra needs one such prophetic figure who is unafraid to blaze away about beliefs in music: too many of them would, of course, become impractical.

Maurice Murphy, on the other hand, red-faced, twinkly eyed, dressed head to toe in a spiffy white sports outfit, clearly enjoys all that he has achieved. Maurice is the LSO's knight-at-arms: there is no other instrument that can project with the force of a trumpet. There is something heroic about a man who can live with that power and also that vulnerability. 'Bored to death or frightened to death' is what they say of the trumpet. It is his plight that he may sit there for weeks blowing only accompanying phrases or part of a thickly written line. Still, he must be prepared once every few months to stand out, to give a clarion call so exposed that there is no faking and nowhere to hide if it goes wrong. 'When Maurice is on', they say of him in the LSO, 'he can give you the old chill down the back.' His is one of the voices that John Fletcher listens to most: 'Maurice has this absolutely beguiling way of playing phrases simply and beautifully,' he says. 'Only a musical dunce would not respond to it.' Murphy still has that sweetness of tone he must have had as a cornet player years ago.

In the baroque period, of course, a secret society existed to initiate trumpeters into the art of their instrument, so unbelievably difficult is it to play well. It requires the delicacy and precision of the violin with the physical stamina of the tuba. The stringed instruments have existed in their present form since the seventeenth century. The brass have continued to evolve so that when, for instance, Beethoven wrote 'trumpet in C', he had in mind an instrument that was tuned a whole octave lower. Perhaps on today's trumpet, it is easier to reach the high notes but the richness and darkness that the young Beethoven heard is no longer there. Only a great artist can capture the same mellowness and burnished quality of sound that was originally intended. The trumpet can set the tone of the whole brass section. It is like the first violin of a quartet, the determining factor. The projection of a forte is not the test: to make a hard, strident noise comes easily on a trumpet. It is the player who can unfurl a beautiful pianissimo, who has depth and projection even at the softest point who will forge a richness in the whole section. Good clean technical playing is not enough: unless it also flows, as Maurice's playing does, it will always sound a little square, a little boring.

Maurice Murphy is a natural musician. Anyone who starts musical life as a nipper in a Salvation Army band standing beside his father and grandfather can be relied on to be fairly free of artistic pretence. He likes to pick up the trumpet and blow. It is hard to imagine him standing around the bandroom of the fabled Black Dyke Mills brass band during the five years he was its principal cornet, dissecting swells, slides or the exact significance of a dot. Just as a matter of course, he and Abbado have their run-ins. ('He says he wants soft,' says Murphy, 'so we try everything – the quietest mute, paper bags over the bells and still he says it's wrong . . . it's the wrong kind of soft.') To one, music is as natural as breathing, to the other it is something to be dissected and analysed. It is inevitable that rehearsals are difficult. It is only all right when they are playing and there is no chance to talk about it. In the heat of the concert, they forge musically.

They ought to be incompatible. Abbado comes from a background where there is reverence for music and for a lifetime's learning. Murphy started work at 15 as an office boy with the National Coal Board in Newcastle. He had his last music lesson at 12: 'My dad started me off until then.' He was 26 before he joined a symphony orchestra – the BBC Northern as principal trumpet. He learned his instrument in dingy village band rooms, in evening rehearsals after a long bus ride, and he remembers them all: the Harton Colliery Band, the Crookhall Colliery Band, the Yorkshire Engineering and Welding Company Band, the Fairey Aviation Works Band and then the mighty Black Dyke Mills.

The traditional British bands are rooted in Wales and the industrial North and Midlands, in towns and villages around coal mines or 'dark Satanic mills'. All the longing and bitterness of those who wore away their lives in these surroundings had to go into a band's sound. Music was not a discipline but a solace. Twenty years blowing the cornet in brass bands shape a musician, they are never forgotten.

Maurice Murphy is 48 years old now, a professor at the Guidhall School of Music, making good money with the LSO. The sweetness and the sadness of a life before this one still come through in his sound.

The orchestra arrives in Boston at lunchtime. The atmosphere is still dour. It is a long afternoon before the rehearsal and tonight's concert. The Boston Symphony is the only American orchestra Abbado conducts now that he is principal guest at Chicago. His Mahler Third here last year with the Boston Symphony – repeated in New York's Carnegie Hall – is still remembered by symphony enthusiasts. It was a moving occasion and received as such even by the *New York Times*. A vist to America by Abbado with his own orchestra is an event.

Boston's Symphony Hall will be full tonight. Last time, the LSO brought with them Mahler's Fifth Symphony, a seemingly infallible choice: the famous 'Death in Venice' adagietto, the passion and sensuality. The Fifth Symphony is free of that tricky touch of irony that crops up in the First. It is hard musically to convey deep emotion while at the same time communicating the irony that mocks that very emotion. An actor has his whole face, his words and gestures to convey mixed and ambiguous feelings. In music there is only pure sound. Last time, it turns out, it went very badly in Boston. Last time, it turns out, went very badly in New York too. This then explains the tension on the journey this morning. No one mentions it but few would forget easily that last concert in Boston.

Mahler's Fifth Symphony opens with a lone trumpet call, technically not all that hard to play but a trifle unnerving. Abbado pulled the orchestra together and gave Murphy the sign to play when he was ready: a twenty-five second trumpet solo to open a symphony that lasts an hour and a half. When a note goes wrong, the second before the sound vanishes lasts a lifetime. Maurice cracked that high note and it seemed to go on for ever. In music sometimes there is no recovery. A heart stops, nerve seizes, muscles stiffen so that their very memory of how to play fails. There was not one musician on stage who did not long to obliterate that moment. One note is all it takes sometimes. It can happen to anyone. String players miss notes all the time and no one is any the wiser, but there is no escaping the trumpet call.

Maurice Murphy went wrong and so went the symphony. That was Sunday in Boston; Monday in New York was even worse. By then, the situation had become a real problem. It was here that Claudio showed the best of himself. Could it be, he asked gently, that Maurice's lip was dried out – a side effect of his air sickness pills, perhaps? A car was ordered to take Maurice on to Washington. A cover story, perhaps, but it was exactly right. Confidence is all. As quickly as it went wrong, it was mended. Three years have gone by since then and Maurice is too blunt to pretend that it never happened. When a trumpet misses, other musicians will say of the phrase that it 'broke his nerve'. It needs nerve to play: iron nerves plus sensitivity, a fragile combination.

Maurice Murphy, *Henry Wood Hall, London*

Maurice did not crack that note without warning. That is what he curses himself for now; he knew he was at risk. He had been through a patch during which his playing seemed to him to have come unstuck. It sounded the same to everyone else but he could feel a difference. He could have asked his assistant to play in Boston – actually those in the know thought he might – but he would not be a trumpet player if he could back away. The fact is that the trouble had started in Boston. The Boston Symphony Orchestra was looking for a new principal trumpet and, at the orchestra's expense, Maurice was invited over to audition. A day trip on Concorde, a limousine to meet him: it was the big gesture, a lark after days of working too hard in London recording studios and he could not resist. He had to try out behind a curtain, in itself a disaster for Maurice's kind of musician who needs to reach out to an audience. In the LSO, auditions are relaxed and easy-going; the idea is not to test a player but to get his measure. Technical prowess is but one qualification for a good colleague. In America, the imposition of democracy on auditions has made them both inflexible and cut-throat. It may have been a lark to Maurice but to all the ambitious, conservatory-trained eager beavers who came at their own expense to audition, it was an event prepared and practised for over weeks. When you are a great player, it is hard to go through the machinery, to be faceless and numbered again. He played badly; he felt mauled. He should never have been there and so, perhaps, that cracked note in the Mahler Fifth in Boston was inevitable.

Ironically, it did not matter how the audition turned out; no one who knows him could picture Murphy settling into an American orchestra – the good manners, the formality, the aloofness of management, the tendency to take oneself too seriously. Even the brass section would have felt alien to him: 'Americans,' he says, 'they always want to discuss everything. Mouthpieces, bell size, mouthpipes, backbores, cuts, throats and things. English players just aren't into all that kind of thing. It doesn't work that way with us. You are what you are; you get what suits you and it works or it doesn't work.'

No one refers today to that last visit to Boston, just as no one mentions that this evening's programme is a veritable declaration of war. Bartók's Miraculous Mandarin suite and Mahler's First Symphony, two stunning showcases for the London Symphony. To bring them both at once to Boston has what Americans call *chutzpah:* nerve or cheek. Every musician needs some of it to go out on stage and play. Trumpet players, as it happens, need more than most.

In suite 1409 a huge basket of flowers welcomes the maestro back to the Ritz-Carlton Hotel. Claudio Abbado stands at the sealed window looking down at the distant figures running and playing in the park below him. He brought his 10-year-old son Sebastian here once when he was younger. In his mind's eye, he pictures the two of them there together and remembers how they stole bread from the breakfast trolley to feed the ducks. He is sad and there is about him an utter gentleness. Sometimes, it seems as though everything of the flesh has fallen away, leaving behind an almost El Greco face. The waiter wheels in his lunch: fillet steak and coffee. Tonight, if the concert goes well he will treat himself to smoked salmon and apple pie.

When he travels, there is always a book close by. At the moment he is reading the autobiography of the 1981 Nobel Prize winner, Elias Canetti, another of those octogenarians to whom, in their wealth of experience and unquenched spirit, Abbado looks for confirmation of things he has come to believe in.

Canetti must seem a very kindred spirit: the small imaginative boy, inwardly living out his terrors and fantasies, who later witnessed the collapse of his and other worlds in war. Abbado was 6 in 1939; his mother was jailed at some point during the war, his father was accused of collaboration afterwards. Abbado too has a complicated history. Canetti, a writer who seeks constantly to impose harmony on chaos, touches a nerve in the conductor. He wrote once to the reclusive author in London and was not surprised in the least that he received no reply. He of all people understands how such an artist would shrink from the new contact.

Last year when he hurt his shoulder, a symptom of exhaustion it is said, Claudio went off alone to the two-roomed family home in Switzerland. It is right at the end of a long valley with no approach road so that the only way in is on skis or by horse-drawn sled. For weeks on end, he sat there in front of the fire, read and skied. 'In the mountains there is no time. When I am working there is always a time limit, airplane time, rehearsal time, it never stops. It is important to find space in your life sometimes, to study and to restudy and to be out of this very crazy life.'

He did not work that time for four months: everything was cancelled, Milan, London, Berlin, Vienna. Not many conductors could afford such a clean sweep, however great the pressure. Outgoings, in this business, have a way of leap-frogging constantly over income. A quarter of a million pounds a year for a top conductor is not an unreasonable income but it soon disappears. Perhaps the artistic temperament does not lend itself to being careful; money, like talent and love, is thought to be limitless in its supply. First-class travel, luxury hotels, lavish apartments, post-concert dinners for twenty at restaurants around the world: it all adds up. So too do the gigantic telephone bills. In the years he has been music director of the Israel Philharmonic, Zubin Mehta has only once put anything in writing to Tel Aviv, in place of simply reaching for the phone. His one exception was a telex sent from some inaccessible region of India. It read: 'This is the telex I never sent you.' Sure enough in Abbado's hand now are three long-distance telephone messages from Zubin Mehta.

Abbado has changed in his five years with the LSO. 'Sometimes in the past maybe I was not free enough,' is all he will say. The odd window has opened in his ivory tower; he understands much more clearly how life is for others and he makes allowances. 'It's so difficult, the musical life for LSO musicians – film work, commercials, they need that to live but I hope one day they'll have a normal life and not have to work like pigs. There's not a great discipline with them like Chicago or Vienna but the point always is "how is the concert?". And in the concert these musicians give a lot and finally that is what counts.'

He needs to rest. Larry Tucker will soon arrive to drive him to the rehearsal at Symphony Hall. Does the orchestra realize that he plans to use every minute of the scheduled two hour rehearsal? Rehearse till seven, concert at eight. In this crazy life, as he says, there is always that old enemy, time.

Backstage at Symphony Hall, in a series of rabbit warrens and narrow burrows, the musicians are changing into tails, claiming their instruments from the storage trunks and going through the pantomime of abusing and insulting them. Nerves take many forms. Someone has hidden himself away in a room to practise: Duggie Cummings, the wild and exuberant principal cello, 'one of the expressions of this orchestra' as Claudio calls him. Duggie must feel pressured to be practising within earshot of his colleagues. Practising is a man's private communication with his instrument. It is also the cosmetic part of playing: covering up the wrinkles, experimenting with new fingering for a passage that is always out of tune, trying a new bowing direction for a note that squeaks or rasps. The way a man struggles to improve is his own secret, which he does not want to give away.

Over in a corner, a cherubic, round, very English face is looking distinctly grey. A couple of the orchestra's old-timers find a moment to cheer him up. 'Just get it in perspective, lad,' says Will Lang, principal trumpet until 1962. The lad is obviously one of the boys, but when he speaks the voice is unmistakable. It is Neville Marriner all over again. Who could miss it? Neville's voice matches his music-making: spritely and unsentimental, the bite, the humour, the attack that is clean but incisive. It has all the qualities of the orchestra he founded and conducted: the Academy of St Martin-in-the-Fields. No one could have this carbon copy of his speech except Andrew Marriner, Neville's son. His father is in Minneapolis now – he is music director of the Minnesota Orchestra – so there have been long phone calls since Andrew and the LSO arrived in America. Neville played second fiddle in the London Symphony for years; he still belongs, in a way, which probably explains why the orchestra can give him a bad time when he comes back to it to conduct. It is not always easy to accept the success of the bloke on the next stand. Neville with his wicked, impish tongue and stylish elegance is the LSO's most famous alumnus along with Barry Tuckwell and Gervase de Peyer. And now here is his son, after years of studying clarinet with Hans Deinzer in Hanover and freelancing around London. He is guest principal for

Douglas Cummings, *Usher Hall, Edinburgh*

the tour, sounding just the right note as an LSO insider: 'It's marvellous fun playing here, getting a crack at the tunes, watching Claudio carve, playing with Dad's mates from when he was in the band. Christ, I used to sit on Will Lang's knee and pick out the horses for him.'

The Cockney note with which he covers up his smart English background is understandable: he has spent years trying to be his own musician, not just 'Nev's boy'. It might have made sense long ago to stay in London and to study with Jack Brymer, the LSO's absent principal, another of that legendary circle of British wind players. But Neville Marriner was still based in London then and a famous father is a mixed blessing. Because of him, some cannot wait to do you down while others cannot wait to cultivate you. Last night in Washington was Andrew's first time out with Abbado: he has passed the conductor's stringent test. 'That clarinet has fantasy' was the report. A compliment indeed, even if, or especially since, Abbado did not get his name. That is not unusual: one violinist has been in the orchestra for seven years and still when Claudio needed to notice him in rehearsal the other day, he could not put a name to him.

Andrew Marriner is still far from at ease: he is bothered by the new mouthpiece he was forced to go with when his old favourite broke a week or so ago. He is worried too that his new reed will not speak. Oboists make their own reeds so that their playing lives are obsessed with the quest for the perfect one. Clarinettists, who can buy theirs ready-made, are spared that particular piece of madness but a major concert such as Boston brings out all their incipient insecurities. In worrying about his reed, Andrew Marriner is just avoiding the real issue of how he will play under tonight's pressure.

How unfair it seems to a wind player: whenever the leader or first cellist has even a small phrase to play alone, it is a special moment, usually signalled as such for bars beforehand. It is a rare leader who can, like Mike Davis, simply pick up the fiddle and play when his turn comes. Such a solo is more usually preceeded by all manner of shuffling and fidgeting, tightening of the bow hair, and pressing the page flat on the stand with the bow tip. And yet every time a principal wind player is on stage there will be many such solos for him, often longer, harder, more crucial to the development of the piece. They have to be taken for granted: no fidgeting in the chair for the principal bassoon before his big solos tonight, just a lot of the spitting and cleaning that reed players go in for. To each man his own nervous twitch.

Friday evening concert, Boston

Musicians do not always know when it will go well. Sometimes they do: there is a friskiness in the air which racehorses would recognize. Tonight there is the usual heavy resignation about the long rehearsal, reviews of the standard of food in Brigham's ice cream parlor over the road (as bad as Henry Wood is the consensus) and some brooding about the prospect of rain and the absence

Backstage at Carnegie Hall, New York with Claudio Abbado and Kurt-Hans Goedicke

of buses. It has been thought healthy for the LSO to try walking to the nearby hotel. The LSO as a rule hates everything represented by the word 'healthy'.

The absence of Boston Symphony players backstage has been generally remarked. At least in Washington, the National Symphony was away on tour in Japan. The Boston Symphony played at home this afternoon with Seiji Ozawa: Bruckner's Eighth to the blue-haired subscription set, hardly the ideal combination. How guest conductors dread the American Friday afternoon audience pitter-pattering in its white gloves, sighing only for 'dear Yehudi' and the Mendelssohn Violin Concerto. Strangely, the one BSO musician who has been glimpsed bringing good wishes is Doriot Anthony Dwyer, the doyenne of American flautists who appeared to arrange a drink with Peter Lloyd, her LSO counterpart. 'Strangely' because unlike other instruments, the flute clans of the world do not get together as a rule. Something in the nature of the instrument, perhaps, that makes them competitors rather than colleagues? 'She's supposedly a very tough lady,' says Peter Lloyd, 'but I've always got on with her. Of course she knows she's good and we English always find that hard to take.'

By the time Michael Davis walks out for his bow, the hall is packed. There is hardly an empty seat anywhere. There is a long, quiet pause before Abbado comes on and the gigantic wave of cheering that then greets him is the first tip-off. It will be stunning or disastrous, all or nothing. Such tension in a hall will either fire an orchestra or set it on edge. Bartók's Miraculous Mandarin suite is another of those 'real Claudio pieces': a brothel, sadism, seduction, beauty, the strange mandarin enticed by the young whore, excited yet cold and impassive. The macabre atmosphere tears through the orchestra; every solo is phrased with heightened emotion and imagination. No one tonight is just sitting and playing the notes in tune. The violins may not match the famous richness of the Boston Symphony but, to be frank, compared to the number of great old Italian instruments in American sections, they are playing on old boxes for the most part. A top American concertmaster would not be playing a nice but unexciting Vuillaume as Mike Davis does; the orchestra board would find a way for him to have a great violin, he would be lent one or lent the money to buy one. But what the LSO does have tonight is an intensity and fervour that a more complacent orchestra might come to only with difficulty.

Abbado, who seemed over lunch so like an invisible cipher, is mesmerizing. When the suite finishes, there is that kind of immediate hullaballoo that takes everyone by surprise. It is like an explosion. This is not an act to be followed easily but the Mahler is still ahead. It is another stunning performance. Duggie Cummings plays his cello as if he has been electrified: his bow arm digs into the strings, his left hand races up and down the fingerboard. His section springs to life behind him each time he lifts the bow. All the tickling that goes on to spare tired left hands is forgotten.

The Fellini-esque third movement, with its eerie atmosphere of the night of the living dead as more and more instruments wander in, produces that silence in the hall that in its concentration is louder than any number of coughing fits, programme notes being noisily if intensely digested, sweets being unwrapped. There is one point in the symphony where Mahler, thorough as he was, says that if the tuba 'cannot bring out his deep note', it should be given to the contra-bassoon. John Fletcher, that tuba virtuoso, comes in with an attack that is so softly covered, it is uncanny. There is simply no way of distinguishing where his note began. The playing throughout the symphony is on this level.

Abbado never lets up, not for a split second. How does he keep such energy and concentration going? He gives power to the performance but it is not a driving, forcing power for he never pushes the tempi. He is like a champion skier in an inspired race leaning always a little too far into the abyss.

When the Mahler is over, there is that split second of silence that is the greatest of all ovations. The cheering that follows goes on and on. It is not last night's well-mannered standing ovation in Washington, the automatic response to a star event. It is the gut response of people who have first been moved and cannot help themselves from showing it. The 'high' backstage afterwards is something tangible. There is a feeling that always follows a great performance: where did it come from? Will it ever, ever come again? Within minutes, despite everything, the orchestra has changed and not a player dawdles behind. Only Abbado stands in his dressing room, patiently receiving every visitor. He greets everyone with the same sweet, shy smile. He hurries no one along. (What a contrast this is to an old pro working a dressing room scene. He would have them in and out in a second and woe betide the lingerers.) When the room finally empties and the strangers have gone, his first question comes, all worry and concern: 'Were the brass too loud?'

That night the waiter delivers to suite 1409 in the Ritz-Carlton a large order of apple pie with an extra serving of cream.

Monday evening concert, New York

Footnote Three nights later, the London Symphony Orchestra plays at Avery Fisher Hall, New York. Donal Henahan, senior music critic of the *New York Times*, reviews the concert. He takes to task 'a few cracked notes in the brass at various times during the night, as well as some surprisingly shaggy work by principals'. One comment, though, should make the orchestra proud. 'Rather than merely a weakening of the sound', he writes, 'a true pianissimo was achieved, which is not as commonly heard from important orchestras as you might imagine.' There are other compliments but this is the best of rewards. Ah, but if only he had been in Boston.

5: Tales from Home

Benjamin Davis is eight years old. He went to school this morning wearing his thickest trousers as a precaution – the small matter of a stink bomb let off yesterday. That is another addition to the list for Ben's dad when he gets home. This list was not looking very good before the stink bomb, it should be said. So far, it includes the information that Ben's bike tyres were ruined and that a broken window at the back of the house cost £64 to repair. It is still more than likely that all such misdemeanours will be overlooked when the time comes. There are plans for a special welcome-home dinner with a turkey, 14 year old Sarah's best pudding and a bottle of champagne. Dad's blue Rover will have been cleaned out and spruced up. Mum is counting on some spells on the sun bed and at the hairdresser's. So in the noise and distraction of the homecoming of Michael Davis, LSO leader, much of what has happened in his absence in this eventful semi-detached in Whetstone will disappear. Five weeks is a long time in family life.

Other things will disappear too, forgotten in the general hubub: the excitement over Sarah's first tennis match for the under 15s ('Great, you're ready for it,' said her mother, 'but play well or don't do it at all. You know that's what dad would say.') There was that special weekend up North and the long visit from grandparents. It is the way it goes these days. For the last four years, Mike has worked for the LSO almost every day of every week and inevitably many of the details of growing up are missed as they never had to be when he led the Hallé Orchestra in Manchester. There then used to be two whole days at home each week: no need when he was around to invoke his name with the weight of a holy presence. On the family notice board next to communiqués from schools, doctors and dentists is the London Symphony's schedule for the world tour. Somewhere in Hong Kong – or maybe it is Bangkok today – the LSO leader is sitting in a hotel room warming up for yet another *Miraculous Mandarin*. The incomplete picture does not seem to fit: how can someone so familiar be so far away and in such unfamiliar surroundings? Is the hotel seedy or exotic? Limply hot or icy cold? What happens, of course, is that when he is away he ceases to have an existence of his own. To the children the only reality is here at home, amid the polished wood, the big Sanderson fabrics, the green velvet chesterfield, the print of the first green at Muirfield Golf Course – familiar objects collected over the years together, the stuff of family life.

When Susan Longson and Michael Davis met, he was 14 and one of the stars of the Pyegrove Tennis Club. Two years later he left school and went to London to the Royal Academy; his life since then has been music and the small wooden box on which he makes it. It was Sue who went on to teachers' training college in Barnes and who first had a career. When they married 16 years ago, he was just going home to join the Hallé while she worked as a qualified teacher. It is easy to imagine how it seemed then: Sue, slender, blonde and pretty, worldlier than he, more independent and able to laugh at things – his buffer against the older men who had always had so much influence over his life, his supporters but also his teachers.

She was not a violinist herself but after enough time together she came to know his playing, perhaps better than anyone. He would ask what she thought about one bowing versus another, one way of phrasing over another. They do not share his music that way nowadays. There is no time and his face is turned not towards the family but towards the orchestra. It is inevitable; he has gone out into the world. She is left to sit through Ben's violin lessons and to supervise his practising. 'Picking my way through that minefield,' is how she puts it. Once again she is a buffer, this time between husband and son, against the expectations of the one and the independence of the other.

The LSO may control her life but her involvement with it is mostly oblique: trying to hear a concert at least once a week; making sure that none of the children bring friends home on concert days; keeping the house quiet during Mike's routine pre-concert naps, reading the schedule to find out where he will be and when. Who would have imagined years ago that he would one day set off for five weeks to a world in which she has no part? When they lived in Manchester, she too had a role and was known by it. Now she is another LSO wife, another faceless Penelope waiting by her tapestry in North London. 'Do you think I'm a poor, weak person?' she asks drily. 'I know a lot of the orchestra do.' It seems so incompatible at times: the hum-drum private life that a family builds and treasures and that other public one carried on amid a hundred strangers. However strong the ties, so much happens in both that, once missed, it cannot be shared: the special concerts, the day off in Hawaii, the flat string in Japan, Duggie's fantastic Elgar concerto in Sydney – and in Whetstone, Ben's stink bomb and the night he could not sleep for fear of being smacked at school.

So much of a family's relationship depends on taking things for granted but after a long tour like this, it is at best uneasy, everyone needs time to settle down together again. It seems such an effort to have to reach out from one world into the other. Mike will have been living on the edge of performance nerves for five weeks, playing out the heightened drama of Mahler and Bartók. There will not be much energy left over for absorbing the goings-on in the garden or even caring about them. Hannah, 9, is interested in her outsize pink panther, her dolls and drawings – will she really want to sit through tales of the first violins' doings in Kuala Lumpur?

There are two versions of a long tour: the first involves some poor, hard-done-by chap, lonely, tired, working hard to keep those at home in comfort. The other pictures an overgrown child, spoiled, fêted, living it up on room service and excitement, who is never around when he is needed. Both seem equally as true at any given moment. After all the anticipation, such a homecoming must always be tricky. 'When Mike's here', says his wife, 'we all move up a gear – there's always more pressure. He gets very screwed up and will come home in the evening and swear and scream until he gets it all out of his system. When he comes in, the routine is to open a bottle of wine, then he paces up and down and we talk while I make dinner. Once he's got rid of it, then he can get into the kids. But after a long tour, he's always changed a little bit – he's definitely a little more abrasive and he swears almost every other word. There's a hard shell that seems to have come round him and it takes time to mellow: but then they have to be hard to survive.'

Orchestras are such old-fashioned, structured affairs – democracy is, after all, only a question of being able to choose who will give the orders – that it is hard for orchestra wives not to slip into old-fashioned and structured ways themselves. At the very least, someone has to make the effort, someone has to take the time to keep things together. Those engaged with the Resurrection, the Ode to Joy, Death and Transfiguration etc. are not much given to remembering plumbers, dry cleaners or just getting the meat into the oven on time. 'As a musician's wife,' says Sue Davis, 'you're very much an appendage, you're not able to be yourself at all. I make a point of never getting upset if anyone ignores me – it just can't be allowed to matter. I hope to go back to teaching and I'll really enjoy it but with three children and our lives such as they are, it's going to be hard. I can't bear it if I know that I've got a pile of ironing waiting to be done and, anyway, it's difficult enough now with four people in the house already all leading different lives.

'Mike gets very cross if he doesn't know where I am. He likes to visualize me here digging the garden, washing the pots and then it's wonderful. I wouldn't exactly say Mike is demanding but it's close. If he has a 10 o'clock rehearsal, you can't be sick at 9 can you? I've never been really sick – well, I do remember once and Mike's immediate reaction was "Where's your mother?"

'His children and his home mean a great deal to Mike but he'll commit himself one hundred and fifty per cent to the LSO – against the family, against everything. A concert with Abbado at the Festival Hall reigns supreme in our house. Nothing, but nothing interferes with it. That is the ultimate.'

Halfway up a steep old farm road on the outskirts of Croydon, a small black and white house stands in a clearing, hidden by thick woods. Badgers have been tearing up the lawn outside the living room window. Orange, yellow and salmon-pink azaleas blaze on huge old bushes. There are 80 foot horse

Playing Stockhausen's Brücken, *Barbican London*

Edward Downes, Claudio Abbado and James Judd *during the filming of the production of* Brücken *by the BBC at the Barbican*

chestnuts, beech, silver birch, pine, ash and may trees, lilac in bloom, rosemary and lavender. This is Jack Brymer's special patch; he does it all himself. Gardening, according to his wife Joan, is a great antidote to 'all that airy-fairy stuff'. She means life as principal clarinet in the LSO.

Jack is the only LSO principal who is not playing on the world tour. That no one bullied him over it is the one concession made to both his age and his stature: neither of which is much talked about. He is 68: middle-aged for a pianist; old for a windplayer. 'Lucky to be around and still perpendicular', as he puts it. He is indeed distinguished: incredibly, all three of his recordings of the Mozart clarinet concerto are still available (Marriner and the Academy, Colin Davis and the LSO and, his personal favourite, Beecham and the Royal Philharmonic from 1958). He has recorded the Firebird six times with four different orchestras. 'I've got to the point now of hearing my own playing with an orchestra I've forgotten I ever played with.' So when Jack said that Joan was not up to it, that was the end of the matter. Everyone knows that Jack goes nowhere without Joan. 'I am very, very old', says Mrs Brymer, flashing her pink pearl nails, violet eyes, five golden rings and inclining her famous pink coiffure, 'and I'm simply rattling with pills.' Jack Brymer is, outwardly, as nice and as plain as his name; in their family, it is his wife who has the bright plumage and blood pressure.

Neither of them, as it happens, fancied Japan or Australia or Hong Kong again. They have done it all so often before. In the early summer, when his garden is alive with colour, Jack does not like the idea of being abroad for five weeks. 'I thought we were going to feel desperately lonely and *de trop* when the orchestra went,' says Joan 'but we've been very busy at dear little festivals in country churches.' There have been three more performances of his beloved Mozart concerto to add to the several hundred he has played in his time: Brighton, Winchester and one at the Royal Festival Hall with the Academy of St Martin-in-the-Fields. Solo engagements are the perks of being what Joan calls 'a little bit famous'. (Jack's 'Mainly for Pleasure' programmes on BBC Radio 3 made him the best-known orchestra member – probably he still is.) Fees are her territory: negotiating them and, later, seeing why they have not been paid. 'Jack's solo fee is only £300. People always say, "Oh, you are cheap!" There was one awful time that the NatWest Bank thought a case of wine would do instead. I'm afraid I got on the phone and I wasn't at all nice. The man there said, "Well, Humphrey Lyttleton the jazz musician did it for nothing!" I ask you, to mention him in the same breath. The whole attitude is so disrespectful. It was very nasty.'

The nasty stuff is always up to Joan. Jack is a clarinettist through and through; his instrument is the prince of the orchestra. There are some things a prince must be above. It is interesting to look around his garden: it has a careless abundance, it is very natural. There is nothing strained, forced or over-manicured; not a fussy corner anywhere. And that is the way he plays the clarinet. Some musicians need to take apart every phrase note by note, to work it over and then to put it back together. Jack's co-principal, Roy Jowitt, is something of a worrier, always going home with music to practise. Jack's great joke about him, with which he never fails to make himself laugh, is that Roy is a man who even practises the Beethoven Seventh. A hearty guffaw: not much to do in that symphony. The fact is, of course, that Jack never practises. His playing has simplicity and beauty, there is nothing artificial about it. He suits the clarinet – it is so much less tortured than the oboe. It is more open and friendly and because of that, it can be more directly compelling. Jack is still at his best in something like Dvořák's Eighth Symphony where the clarinet solos with their special 'woodsiness' of tone quality give the music that autumnal, nostalgic feeling. He is the last of a generation; they call it old-fashioned now, of course.

It is very curious how fashions of playing change. Young violinists listening to old recordings of long-ago heroes will wince at the slides, the 'soupiness' and sentimentality. Pianists strive for ever more fearsome fingers; time enough at 80 to court the epithet 'limpid'. And newer clarinettists play with a more concentrated sound than Jack's, with less vibrato; it is harder and tougher than his. And they could, probably, play rings around him now when it comes to the spunkiness of the instrument – Till Eulenspiegel's hanging given by Richard Strauss to the clarinet or the leering, devilish E flat clarinet part at the Witches' Sabbath in Berlioz's *Symphonie Fantastique*. The clarinet is, in its way, a much more youthful sounding instrument than a horn or oboe – firm and muscular. In the funeral march in Beethoven's Eroica, two clarinets playing one note in unison can dominate the stage in the midst of full fortissimo string writing. But the instrument also has its special note of melancholy and of beauty: the old school (Jack calls it 'vocal'), could float a phrase so that it hurt. He still can.

Who can say whether a musician comes to have the character of his instrument and of the music written for it or whether the instrument itself attracts a matching personality? In Jack's case, he has lived with the clarinet for 64 years since he first climbed on to a stool as a small boy in South Shields to sneak off with his father's Sunday instrument from the drawer. He has the clarinet's geniality and it is all too easy to be misled by it: by the talk of the 18 handicap at golf, the dashing about on his Honda in a bright red catsuit, the straightforwardness of playing ('There is no secret to making a beautiful sound'). He plays from a more complex source than he talks. 'I think', he says, 'that by striving for complete perfection in music, you kill a work. Very often we're striving for cold perfection when I'm pretty certain that a warm, musical feeling is what we're after.' It is not surprising that he cites violinist Fritz Kreisler as one of his musical heroes: 'Such deep humanity, such marvellous musical enjoyment'. Not for Brymer the steely, restrained, almost superhuman qualities of Jascha Heifetz.

But it is this very geniality that has seen him through a long career without the crabbiness so characteristic of many of his older colleagues. If this week's recording session with Barbra Streisand had its grim aspects, he would rather talk of what a charmer Michel Legrand, the French pop composer, turned out to be. He has been focusing on the good side for many years now: he has had to. Like so many musicians, he knew the best at the very beginning of his career – it never again had that glow, that sense of discovery. For him the golden days were the 1950s: in Sir Thomas Beecham's new and last orchestra, The Royal Philharmonic – Denis Brain as first horn, Terence MacDonagh as first oboe, Jack as first clarinet. There were those early summer-long seasons at Glyndebourne. Was it really the musical idyll that legend and his memory has it? Or is it that those who remember it were young then when everything is at its best and finest? There is no way of knowing for recording techniques have changed too much. Besides, those who in America look to Toscanini's NBC Orchestra as the greatest days of music, and those who in London talk of Beecham are, in their way, yearning for another world, not only for another way of making music.

Mrs Brymer is very grand; she talks in the first person plural (as in 'we will be playing' and 'our concerts') but she has forged for herself a role as the LSO's Queen Mum. The musicians are the children she no longer teaches, they are the one son now in his thirties whom she remembers as that soft, small boy in the faded grey photograph albums by the Magicoal fire in the living room. She sees herself as part of the orchestra. 'I can't resist them; I miss them when they're not here like this – although sometimes when I'm on tour with them, I'm not sure I *can* love them any more. Jack always gets into trouble with me for not bringing home more personal news. I say, "So what did he say" and "what did he have to eat?" And he says: "I didn't notice."

'For a while, I used to scrape away myself at the back of the violas in the Croydon Symphony – I would invite all the neighbours in to hear me doing my thing and they'd all laugh – but it means that I do know how hard it is. I do think the orchestra laughs at me. I often see people nudging each other but I like my pink hair – I used to be mauve – and when it comes to clothes, I'm deeply sure of myself. I don't give a couple of jam jars what anyone says about me or thinks about me. I'm old and I'm just doing my thing.'

Mrs Jack Brymer is longing for the LSO to come home now and for any scrap of news about how the tour has gone. Every morning she glances at this doormat: a postcard perhaps? Just a word to say that they are not forgotten, maybe even missed ? It never comes of course.

Gaia Servadio Mostyn-Owen, her husband Willy and their younger son, Orlando, are having a bite of supper in the kitchen: cucumber salad, taramasalata, fresh mozzarella, fish and rice, pumpkin, zabaglione, halva, quinces, a few plump cherries. Orlando is 10 and much preoccupied with the

At Windsor Castle

new Covent Garden production of Puccini's *Manon Lescaut* on television. Willy, head of Christie's Old Masters department, runs through a list of acquaintances in America with the casualness of one who assumes that everyone knows 'old this' who runs that, or 'old that' who runs this. Gaia, a little weary after last week's shindig in Kuwait and this week's trip to Oslo, sighs for the thought of summer in their Shropshire family home.

She mentions that daughter Allegra is off to Sri Lanka and India for six weeks on Wednesday. Ah, it seems only yesterday that Allegra and Owen, then 10 and 8, went off with Gaia to Estonia and Russia for one of her books, *A Siberian Encounter*. ('Anybody can go to Siberia – they weren't very jolly months, of course.') It is heady stuff, a very rich mixture indeed. The house itself has a vibrant feeling: scarlet and emerald walls, paintings, masks, postcards, collections of old teapots, photographs of extraordinarily beautiful children growing up. One of these shows Orlando with his special friend, Sebastian Abbado: they are at school together, they stay over at one another's houses, in a way they are both 'only children'. It is but one thread of an intricate connection.

Gaia is one of the Abbadisti, the henchmen of Abbado. Round every large musical figure there develop these clusters of friends, stationed around the world, who, taken all together, give a semblance of unity to a peripatetic life. They meet after concerts, wherever business or pleasure takes them: Paris, London, Milan, Salzburg, Bayreuth. They are drawn together by the artist at their centre and soon come to look quite comfortable moving together in a pack between choice seats in the stalls and backstage in intermission. There are stellar musicians who seem to seek out the most ordinary of companions notable for their drab, devoted faces, bad hairdressers and tailors. Is it to make sure that there is one haven in life free from competition, pretence or appearances? Others, like Abbado, look for sparkle and relief: for Italian (it is tiring to live always in other languages), for style, effervescence, confidence. In London, there are Gaia Servadio, Franco and Raimonda Buitoni of the pasta Buitonis, John Leech and his Italian wife, Noretta, from the City and Chester Square. It is a small select group given to sheltering Claudio and knowing how to do so with more discretion and a lighter touch than most.

All too often, it is easy to spot the privileged circle of a Great Artist: they look so much more pleased with themselves than anyone else backstage. Artists must perform, managers must book. Friends have other less nerve-racking responsibilities. Part entourage, part guardians, they run errands, chauffeur, carry bags, find staff, monitor rehearsals, organize parties, close dressing room doors, book tables, recommend choice hotels and, above all, care deeply and often. In time, they see it as their particular job to shield the great man from the intrusion of Philistines: a category, alas, that can come to include everyone not known to and approved by their tight inner circle. Wives, newer ones especially, are not immune to disapproval. No artist is ever treated well enough; it is up to the protectors to watch out for him.

The Abbadisti are brighter than most and not given to such airs and graces. Just as well: their group embraces not only Claudio but the Jesuitical figure of pianist Maurizio Pollini, another of the Italian 'family'. Not much scope for pretentious or possessive green room behaviour with him. Gaia is a friend of both: the driven and shy Pollini, the gentler and childlike Abbado. Evidently, she and Willy know how to make them feel safe – a rare gift. They go back a long way together: it is ten years now since Gaia was able to put a word into the correct Communist Party circles in Italy on Claudio's behalf to help push a troubled La Scala-Covent Garden exchange. Now she is arts' correspondent for *La Stampa*, the influential Turin newspaper; as such she appreciates the minutiae of musical politics as well as the artistry. She also gives after-concert parties for Claudio when he so wishes: softly lit, velvety suppers, seemingly effortless. They are rich, elegant and yet cosy. A world away from anything the LSO stands for.

Most orchestras ignore the chosen circle around a music director. They take for granted its whispering, gossiping and sly criticisms. The LSO, rather astutely, realized early on that the Abbadisti were another of Claudio's assets and, as such, should not be allowed to go to waste. The right wife has long been seen as part of a conductor's volunteer staff (it goes down very well in Chicago, for instance, when Gabriella Abbado appears with Claudio and Lady Solti is famed there for her winning ways with the ladies' committees). Soon after Abbado took over the LSO from Previn, the LSO Executive Committee came into being: 'To advance the interest of the LSO in the world of business, government and politics, and to stimulate an awareness of its contribution to artistic life', as the official statement has it.

Gaia, John Leech and Franco Buitoni are members, there to interpret Claudio when necessary, to let it be known when he is 'feeling intimately offended', as Gaia puts it. They are there, too, to cajole him into some piece of public relations when they (but not he) see the point of it. The committee, inevitably, has come to have a life beyond Claudio. Its chairman Bernard Donahue, formerly of 10 Downing Street (under Harold Wilson) and *The Times*, is something in stockbroking. From Eaton Square came financier and politician Lord Lever. The 'cashmere leftists' of London SW1 bring to the LSO their particular expertise, their understanding of worldly matters and an extensive list of influential acquaintances. The attempt to cultivate the drawing rooms of London must be working: the Philharmonia Orchestra has followed suit with its own small group. An orchestra may sleep in North London; it must learn to smile in smarter places.

Supper is over. Orlando and Willy are off upstairs to watch Manon die in Louisiana. Allegra will be home soon from Les Ambassadeurs. On Gaia's desk there are papers, invitations, half-finished drafts and a diary full of engagements. LSO comes home this week – Gaia had quite forgotten.

6: The Salzburg Connection

Saturday morning

Another airport; another queue. It is seven o'clock in the morning and some things look reassuringly familiar: Sue Mallet stands at the elbow of a British Airways official chivvying him along. She has discovered a way of boarding the LSO's chartered plane in the absence of air tickets. These have vanished in the British Airways computer. 'It's disgusting really', she says blithely, 'how disorganized they are.'

There are, however, telling differences. Almost everyone seems fatter than they were two months ago in America. Faces are fuller. Instead of the everyday LSO look, grey and haunted, there is now a long line of robust and ruddy cheeks. Compared to their usual rumpled state, the musicians look well-dressed. There are natty new jumpers that fit and trousers that have yet to acquire the standard quota of spots. There is a holiday air about and, indeed, the orchestra has just had a week off. Unintentionally, as it turns out. There should have been a trip to Greece for the Athens festival but it fell through. Cancellations: there is an epidemic of them these days.

The chaps of the LSO, an incorrigible mixture of doom and optimism, have no particular sense of foreboding. The summer always seems a bit slack and things are always falling through. Forward schedules, even for the next month, are famous for their use of the word 'possible' – as in 'poss. recording', 'poss. film', 'poss. concert'. Some will doubtless be making appointments to see the bank manager in the near future for they always glide too close to the edge. The summer days have been hot and sunny; there have been outings with children, camping trips, sailing or just hours of basking in the garden. How ordinary everyone looks once the special edge of exhaustion has been smoothed away. For a week, the war was over. The LSO now looks worryingly peaceful: worryingly, because as an orchestra it plays traditionally on its nerves and BA 9343D dep: 7.55 is flying to Salzburg, the most prestigious event in the international music calendar.

Salzburg is music's Field of the Cloth of Gold. It is where the great alliances and treaties of music are made and sealed. The presidents and managing directors come themselves to Salzburg; there is no relying on the number two man here. He can keep watch over Glyndebourne or Aix-en-Provence. At any given moment in favoured restaurants – the Goldener Hirsch or Gasthof zum Hirschen at Parsch – will be gathered that handful of music's power

David Hume and Bruce Mollison, *Avery Fisher Hall, New York*

brokers and superstars. Opposite the concert hall, in a bijou garden suite of offices, Deutsche Grammophon makes its summer pilgrimage from Hamburg. All the top brass will be here. There is a story told of a famous conductor who was finally invited to perform at Salzburg. A few minutes before he went on stage, an official came to greet him. 'Well,' asked Herr Doktor Official without a glimmer of a smile, 'are you ready for Salzburg?'

It is the birthplace of Mozart and the summer resting place of Herbert von Karajan. It is hard to think which of the two is believed to be of greater consequence. Most musicians, however respected or fawned upon, are in the end at the mercy of others, the toys and puppets of richer, stronger forces. Without patrons or government support, there would be no musical arena for them. Herbert von Karajan is a law and an industry unto himself. It is said that single-handedly, he accounts for 40 per cent of Deutsche Grammophon's turnover. This is power indeed. When other musicians joke about him – and, revealingly, that is not often considering that humour is music's universal language – it is usually some reference to his standing in Heaven. It is some variation on the story about a lofty conductor who will talk only to God – and, when he does, von Karajan answers. Salzburg is von Karajan's very own temple. Here all patronage stems from him.

There are only fourteen orchestral concerts during the month-long festival. Seats for them cost £40 each and are sold out by post months beforehand. Only a special few favoured and princely conductors are invited. This year the list includes James Levine from New York's Metropolitan Opera House, Riccardo Muti from the Philadelphia Orchestra, Seiji Ozawa from Boston, Zubin Mehta from New York and Lorin Maazel, general manager of the Vienna State Opera. Most festivals would be glad of the presence of just one of these conductors. Except for Klaus Tennstedt, this season neatly includes every name mentioned as von Karajan's possible successor at the Berlin Philharmonic. (Orchestras love to defy such expectation. In London, the tipsters were astounded by the Philharmonia's invitation to Giuseppe Sinopoli to succeed Muti.)

The Berlin Phil. is here and the Vienna Philharmonic – the two orchestras known to the irreverent as Herbie's bands. They are also described as the standardbearers of European tradition, as if Beethoven and Brahms sat always at their elbow. How ironic that the two greatest of the world's orchestras (although they might not agree with that claim in Chicago or Philadelphia) come from cities of such uneasy political circumstances with musical pasts that have been both glorious and ignominious. It is only because of the flight of all those great musicians and teachers from Vienna and Berlin that music has become so deeply rooted in the orchestras and conservatories of America, where a whole generation has grown up that does not even think of looking to Europe for inspiration.

Every year, one or two outside orchestras are invited to play here. This summer it is the turn of the Israel Philharmonic and the London Symphony. Hard to name two other orchestras that are such an antithesis to the mighty Berlin and Vienna, these latter so weighty, sober and secure. Both the LSO and the IPO play from their instincts and their emotions; both have music directors (Abbado and Zubin Mehta) who go for the raw feeling underneath the passages that they are conducting and therefore bother less than some if all the seams are not perfectly sewn, all the attacks are not together.

Salzburg, then, is an unlikely place for the LSO to do well. It is select to the point of stifling – snobbish, overdressed and formal. Not a ragged note anywhere. To come here is an extraordinary gamble in such hard times. An orchestra honoured by an invitation must not be found wanting; one bad night in Salzburg and the world will know. And besides, Salzburg is as ruinous as any other royal progress upon the chosen. For the privilege of playing two concerts, the London Symphony has had to find £40,000 of sponsorship funding to subsidize the fees. It is part of the absurd irony of running an orchestra at the moment that if only it could avoid playing concerts, it would not run into debt.

But, as always, the chaps carry on with their same endearing capacity for running everything down. Berlioz's *Symphonie Fantastique* again. 'Can play it in my bleeding sleep.' Abbado again. 'Haven't seen him for weeks; haven't missed him either.' There has been a month-long Brahms festival at the Barbican with Rafael Kubelik conducting. He is spoken of now with that particular awe that, in its time, the LSO has reserved for Monteux, Böhm, and Celibidache. Kubelik, son of Czech composer Jan Kubelik, and until recently music director of Munich's Bayerische Rundfunk, has the right combination of encroaching age and rocklike musical independence that seems to inspire the LSO. If it played well on the world tour, it played superbly for Kubelik.

Wholehearted support from serious music critics in London has had an effect. The received wisdom from *The Times* is now that Kubelik 'saved the LSO', that under his guidance the LSO proved itself worthy after all the City of London's continuing support etc. etc. The LSO and its born-again musicians are suitably grateful. They pay tribute to Kubelik's gentleness, to the way he talked to them and discussed matters in rehearsal, to the substance of his interpretations. Everyone says now that the orchestra has not played as well for years.

How odd that this thought should be put into words by the players themselves. It refers, of course, to that golden age of the LSO at the end of the 1960s and the beginning of the 1970s: James Galway among the flutes, Néville Marriner leading the second violins, Gervase de Peyer on clarinet, Barry Tuckwell first horn, Roger Lord as principal oboe, Ernest Fleischmann (that irresistible force now ruling in Los Angeles) general manager. It was a period when the LSO played with uncaring brilliance. It had total confidence in itself; it had no doubt that it was the finest orchestra in London and therefore played as such.

Today's doubts and uncertainties make it an older, wiser ensemble. There are those who believe that as a result it has much more character when it plays well now. There are those who still look back and this shadow of the past is an orchestra's curse. There can be no finite moment in its music-making; there is only the constant search. At times, it does go better. Under Kubelik, a great, old and unfortunately sick bear of a man, it went extraordinarily well. It was a month of digging into the meaning of music again, of feeling anew what it is to be supported by an older man's wealth of experience. It was a month heightened by the knowledge that it might never be repeated. Coming back to Claudio Abbado after such a period of intense discovery and success has all the allure of going home to the wife.

The wife; that's it. There is another reason why the early morning queue at Heathrow Airport looks odd. Salzburg is traditionally an outing for the missus. It is the perfect place to be a tourist, it is not too far from home and, maybe, faced with the pressure to do well there are those who want a bit of moral support. Under the knowing eyes of so many mothers, the LSO lines up demurely in its holiday best. Those who like to see themselves as 'the lads' are suddenly thrown back into their other roles as sober husbands and middle-aged fathers. Wives can be a tricky lot: anyone in music can confirm that. Quick to take offence, to stand on a husband's rights, to defend him against slights, a wife is not a music administration's most popular creature. The only reason girl friends are not made more welcome is that they may all too soon turn into yet more wives.

Sue Mallet spent hours at the last minute poring over the plane's seating plan. Someone's wife joined the party late and insisted on sitting next to her husband. Someone's aged mother-in-law felt like coming too but needed to be right in the centre of town. Accommodation in Salzburg is both hard to find (Sue is having to use twelve hotels) and expensive. More rearranging was required. 'I've managed to put you all together in the Hotel Zum Dom just by the Festspielhaus,' Sue calls out merrily to the flute, his wife, his 86 year old mother-in-law and daughter as she spies them all in the queue before her. 'Oh yes,' nods the gloomy flute, 'I know it. Right by the Cathedral. Won't sleep a wink all night.'

Saturday afternoon
A rehearsal has been called for five o'clock in the Festspielhaus paint shop, an enormous barn of a place, two storeys high, which is reached from the ground floor courtyard by a trundling lift. The gate of this lift clangs loudly each time it opens and shuts, as it will do again and again during the next three hours, usually at the softest point of a pianissimo. No one seems to notice.

A haystack drops stalks near the array of gongs, drums and bells laid out for the percussion. A big Romantic piece is obviously afoot. A detached arm,

Henry Greenwood, *Lenigrad*

a baby's skeleton and a death mask rest near two gigantic open wicker laundry hampers – Henry Greenwood's travelling music library. A mammoth lion's head from *Idomeneo* hangs above the trombones, the prison gate from *Fidelio* rests near the harp cases. Through a heavy metal door in one corner, it is possible to creep on to the workmen's gallery overlooking the Grosses Festspielhaus stage to eavesdrop on Herbert von Karajan's *Rosenkavalier*, talked of this season in Salzburg as a miracle.

Surrounded by all these accessories and reminders, the LSO is trying very hard to pretend that this is just another rehearsal hall and just another concert. The poker face that the orchestra presents to pressure, the pose that nothing matters too much, the desire not to be made too much of – all the lack of fuss is suddenly shown up as a set of carefully cultivated and very good musical manners. The last thing anyone needs right now is an outburst of nerves: the jitters are too contagious.

It is a surprise to watch the musicians come into the shop from the elevator or up the stairwell by the windows. They walk so slowly and seem so unfocused. Usually LSO players are by custom masters of the quick entry. Since they always leave it until the last possible second, they have learned how to cover distances with the least visible movement. An old LSO hand can turn up for a rehearsal one minute before it is due to start and be in place, instrument to hand, right on time without the slightest suggestion of feeling rushed. There is no official penalty for being late in the LSO but any fellow who has endured the shuffling and jeering of his colleagues is unlikely to want to repeat the experience. Within its own idiosyncratic code, the LSO makes much of its professionalism. The reluctant pace today is caused by a sudden self-consciousness and embarrassment. A week is a long time for the LSO not to play together.

Some people have not touched an instrument all through it. They have lost their bearings, that extra sensitivity to one another. Fingers and lips can no longer be trusted. There is always a price to pay for unwinding and it is this reluctance to be wound up again. What a way to turn up at Salzburg. And somewhere there, hidden in the emotional undercurrent, is the complicated response to the sight of Claudio Abbado, stained mahogany brown after a month in Sardinia. He looks lean and young again; it was a *real* holiday. Nothing points up the discrepancy between music's gods and its mortals as much as what the gods are able to do with their time off.

Playing here tomorrow night will be hard on Abbado. He first made his name internationally in Salzburg with a stunning Mahler Second Symphony. It was 1965, he was 32 and one of those 'overnight successes', another von Karajan 'discovery': as if there were ever any overnight successes in a profession in which so many years go into study, preparation and apprenticeship. He has returned to Salzburg many times since then. He is staying at the Hotel Fondachhof, a 200 year old manor in its own park outside town. He has carefully put a distance between himself and the feverish, intricate atmosphere in town.

Salzburg, like Vienna, is a byword for musical intrigue. Abbado is the only conductor, except for von Karajan himself, to conduct two concerts here this year. On the other hand, it is worth looking at the repertoire for the season. What counts in Salzburg is, basically, German and Viennese music, meaty and substantial. Von Karajan is conducting a Brahms cycle, Maazel has the massive Eighth Symphony of Bruckner, Mehta brings Mahler's gigantic Third Symphony; Levine has the Seventh. And Claudio Abbado is bringing French and Russian-French descriptive party pieces. No one, not even a devotee, has ever claimed that Berlioz's *Symphonie Fantastique* and Mussorgsky-Ravel's *Pictures at an Exhibition* are attempts to define the nature of man's existence.

Berlioz's symphony is a repudiation and exorcism (complete with beheadings and witches' sabbath) of the composer's then hopeless passion for an actress. Ravel's orchestration of Mussorgsky's piano piece describes a series of paintings, sketches and sculpture by Victor Hartmann, an artist whose work would be forgotten without this musical catalogue. A Russian witch in flight, two Polish Jews and a great gate of Kiev that was never built: it is hardly the stuff of which immortality is made in Salzburg.

They are more like warhorses – pieces with which to ride into town and conquer. Beethoven's Fifth Symphony is a warhorse, so too is the Tchaikovsky Fifth. Beethoven's Ninth would be, despite its lofty 'brotherhood of man' ideals, were it not so expensive to mount: in Japan where such considerations matter less, it already is a warhorse. In his own lifetime, Stravinsky started to complain that the *Rite of Spring* was being thus downgraded, run through loud and fast for the quick success. Musical snobs (and Salzburg is nothing if not snobbish) do not have much time for warhorses or those hired hands who ride them. And yet, when they come off, the Fantastique and the *Pictures* can be thrilling, for Berlioz and Ravel are among the handful of great orchestral writers who fully grasped the secrets of instrumental scoring. When and if . . . the LSO cannot afford a failure in Salzburg. This is far more of a gamble than it cares to admit.

Everyone talks of how wonderful it is to be back in Salzburg, of how pretty it is in the sunshine. There is another side to it. Near the centre of town, there is a booth advertising coach tour attractions. One board lists the 'Sound of Music' trip, visiting the settings from the film. Another gives details of a day's outing to Berchtesgaden, known best to foreigners as Hitler's mountain retreat: the two faces of Salzburg, the charm of chocolates, pastries and postcard views, the complicated underbelly. Salzburg was bombed during the war and Mozart's birthplace and childhood home have had to be rebuilt. They are the focus of a large tourist industry and at every turn there is a reproduction of the young Mozart's profile: smooth, elegantly wigged, without a care. There can be no pilgrimage to the site of his death; he died in Vienna in 1791 and was buried in an unmarked pauper's grave. There is instead this celebration in Salzburg with its stiff promenades nightly outside the Grosses Festspielhaus and endless boxes of rich chocolate balls, *Mozartküchel*. No mention of the way in which he had to leave this town or the poverty in which he died in another. Salzburg would put most musicians on edge; it is full of ambiguity and ambivalence, which are not conducive to great performances.

Nor can it escape notice for long that in the hundreds of window displays given over to record companies' advertising posters, two faces predominate: Herbert von Karajan for Deutsche Grammophon and Riccardo Muti for EMI.. Their images are everywhere: the one, a silvery mystic, the other, a sultry dauphin. Large television trucks stand outside the Festspielhaus: a film is being made of Muti's *Così fan tutte*.

Deutsche Grammophon is asked why there seem to be two Abbado posters in the whole of Salzburg. In truly German fashion, DG responds with a written list in contradiction: it turns out that there are actually seven locations displaying a photograph of Claudio Abbado. Somehow this pedantic literalism sparks the LSO sense of humour when word gets round. But it is hard for both conductor and orchestra not to feel slighted as they walk the streets, not to feel that there is something to be proved here. It is not an auspicious way to make music.

Given that most audiences like to be eased into a concert with something jolly (Rossini or Haydn, maybe) or rousing (the Rienzi Overture as an extreme), it is probably courageous of Abbado to open tomorrow night with Anton von Webern's Six Pieces, Opus 6. In New York, the audience responded by coughing so loudly that the coughing itself became the subject of the *New York Times* music review. The whole work lasts less than ten minutes; it is stark, rhythmically very complicated and some things in it are incredibly difficult to play. Webern produced his music sparingly note by note – his entire output is not as long as one Wagner opera – and thus the possibilities for disaster are enormous. When two or three notes can ruin the musical substance of almost the whole piece, it takes nerve and technique just to play it. To do so with the right, awesome intensity requires a commitment that not many people have. If audiences resist the idea of austere, modern music, the men who have to perform it are even less enthusiastic. Most orchestras do not think of it as *real* music; to them it sounds 'like dead spiders' legs on tracing paper.'

The LSO does do its best for Webern, if only because the Second Viennese School is another of Claudio's 'things'. But there is pride involved too: in a piece like this which is pure and distilled music, every instrument's contribution is equal. When every note counts and no player is given a drawn-out or even discernible melody, each phrase stands out. It is the moment when the musical skeleton of an orchestra shows up; it reveals those musicians who might normally go unnoticed but who form part of the orchestra's backbone. When there is no fat, no rich, full-blown phrases and pretty tunes, there is more, not less, to hear and see. It is remarkable the way this orchestra's players listen to one another and respond to the tightened structure of the music. Where, in the big set pieces, they are happy to follow Abbado's beat – rather late, as a matter of fact – here they are right with him. However dismissingly they may talk of the music, they react instinctively to its drama. Those who are not playing respect its silences; they do not destroy their impact with fidgeting and rustling. This is more unusual than it might seem.

The flute opens the first movement. It is an awakening to recognize from those few notes how much weight Peter Lloyd, the principal flute, carries in the wind section. It is so easy not to take his instrument seriously – Mozart never did. ('There isn't really much you can do with a flute,' says Peter himself, somewhat morosely. 'It's very dull.') It is tempting for the listener to sit back most of the time and enjoy the flute's flowing tunes, to take for granted Peter Lloyd's full-bodied tone, the imagination with which he answers other instruments' phrasing in the section. It is not often that a flute carries as much musical authority as an oboe or clarinet: indeed, there is a saying in orchestras that it is possible to have a mediocre principal flute and still have a great wind section. In the beginning of the Webern, Peter Lloyd's playing is big and deep; he brings to his few notes a world of expression.

Another such moment comes a little later. The LSO must be the only orchestra in the world that is inspired by its harpist, that holds him in as high esteem as any of its other soloists. Only a special musician would have the imagination, let alone ability, to bring such dynamic colour and range to these few notes in the Webern. It is not easy to make a harp, that celestial accessory of cherubs and angels, take on a character as menacing and full of chill as Osian Ellis brings to it here. It often comes as a surprise to outsiders to learn that Osian Ellis is the LSO's harpist and has been since 1960. His name comes under the heading of those 'musicians' musicians' who are so distinguished that they are assumed to be either dead or decrepit. (Watch foreigners at BBC Symphony Orchestra concerts craning to see a burly, grey-bearded man at the back; they are trying to catch sight of Alan Civil, the great horn player, marvelling that he is there at all.)

Osian Ellis is associated with those magical days of Benjamin Britten's Aldeburgh. He played the last recital tours with Sir Peter Pears after the composer was too sick to travel himself with his old friend. Ellis is the one link in the LSO to the creative source of music: few musicians have the chance as he had to bring life to new music (fewer still want to, of course). To have inspired Benjamin Britten to write for him has produced a lasting legacy for the harp literature. So rare are great composers such as Britten that those who were close to them, those for whom the music was originally written, acquire some kind of immortality of their own. Their names reach across the years: 'Mr Stadler, the elder' for whom Mozart wrote the clarinet concerto; Schuppanzigh, the violinist of Beethoven's quartets; Joachim for whom Brahms wrote the violin concerto, sonatas and double concerto.

It is fitting, then, that Osian Ellis should stand out from his colleagues both musically and sartorially. He looks more solid than most, more of a visiting businessman with his short grey hair and conservative wardrobe. He also seems far more aware, as he looks on with his quick and quizzical eye. But that is the perennial condition of the harpist: to look on and to notice everything that escapes those who play in the thick of it. Orchestra players, as a rule, cannot help but resent the harpist. All that time off, all those lengthy movements during which he sits and watches the others work. Besides, there is something not quite right about the harp: it takes such tremendous strength and coordination – 47 strings, 7 pedals, 3 levels each pedals.

The harp is without a natural ally; it belongs nowhere. It has the most universal function of all the instruments: it can be used as an extension of the string pizzicati as in the Mahler Fifth Symphony adagietto, for instance. Sometimes it can play with the winds, giving literally a little 'ping' to the attack of their notes. There are those sweeping arpeggios for which it is most famous. But it always conveys colour, not emotion. It is, therefore, always the outsider, the observer of the heated weaknesses of others.

Harpists react differently to this isolation. Some delight in it and withdraw into a separate world (literally so in the case of one famous orchestra harpist who used the harp case as a 'hotel room' for changing and brushing up). Others over-compensate with hearty eccentricity. Osian uses his isolation to listen and to take note. Twenty years ago, he was at the heart of the orchestra's politics; now he leaves that to others. He went away for a while building a solo career all over the world but never severed the connection entirely. Two years ago, when he got tired of carrying his harp around himself and paying away most of his fees to others (20 per cent commission; 30 per cent withholding tax in the United States, travelling expenses) he drifted back to the LSO full-time. 'It was a question of loyalty as well. I feel I owe it to the orchestra.'

Sitting here in the paint shop of the Festspielhaus, Osian is clearly fading fast; he is beginning to regret his five o'clock gardening stint this morning before setting off for Salzburg, checking on his dill, spinach, radicchio and lettuce. He would not mention it himself but he was in Salzburg only two years ago to play a solo recital in the Festival. It was sold out. Today, as far as he is concerned, he is just a man without a seat to call his own. The running battle continues to sit somewhere that he can actually hear. '"*They*" like to put you in the back of the second fiddles and I like to sit next to the flutes. You have to fight for it every time and it all depends on what authority you have in the orchestra. Since I'm still fighting, the answer must be "not much".'

Osian Ellis, *Usher Hall, Edinburgh*

A typical LSO piece of self-deprecation. On an instrument generally disdained by its colleagues in orchestras, Osian produces a sound that is unique. In a small part that character is, oddly enough, technical: unlike other harpists, he leaves his long fingernails uncut as the medieval players did and as guitar and lute players still do. It gives him an entirely different palate of sound to work with; he can, physically, bring more subtleties into the colour, more brilliance into an attack. But beyond playing the right notes, in tune, in the right place, he is that rare creature: an orchestra musician for whom his instrument is merely his means of expression within the textural fabric of the whole. It is odd how few orchestra members ever follow a score or study a new piece in its entirety before playing it. They stare at their own part on the stand and it is the limit of their musical world and of their vision. In time most become instinctively aware of others, of listening to and playing with them, but few consciously know why or how the jigsaw puzzle of a piece of music fits together as a whole.

Osian would deny all this; he is enough of an LSO man to talk in an utterly matter-of-fact way about music and his part in it. 'In Welsh villages,' he says, 'if you played the harp it was either because your mother did or because you were a fairy. When I was a boy I played the harp because my mother did, the piano and the organ and that was normal in Wales then.' About ten years ago he took a sabbatical and went off as a fellow to the University of Wales to write the history of the harp in Wales, in both Welsh and English ('Well, it's the history of Welsh music of course'). He thinks of going back there now and again – when he is tired or when he gets fed up with footling about in the back of the orchestra and especially when he has had enough of trying to find the elusive LSO pitch.

They are about to rehearse the Symphonie Fantastique in which the harp does not enter until the second movement. If he takes his A at the beginning of the symphony, he is bound to be flat by the time he comes in. The orchestra warms up and gets excited, the A sharpens. 'If it's hot', he says in a resigned tone, 'the clarinets and bassoons in this orchestra go sharper much more quickly than the flutes, so you have to know exactly who you're playing with.' In the bag by his side is his Salzburg special: a Japanese electronic tuning device. A harp needs all the help it can get. 'I can't complain. Obviously one needs to make music and when you're working in an orchestra you're working on huge canvases which is what attracts me. Besides, I'm philosophical, you see. I take it as it comes. You have to if you play the harp.'

Saturday evening

The rehearsal breaks up. Within seconds, the lift has left on the first of its many trips. At 8 o'clock, it is still burning outside with a heavy, summer heat and, for some, the important part of the day is about to begin. Sitting back and enduring a three hours' rehearsal is seen as the price that must be paid for an evening out in Salzburg. For others, one town is much like another. They are here to play and the free hours are only time to be passed as cheaply as possible.

In one corner, the 'barrow boys' are planning when and where to meet after going back to shower and change. In another, the old style gentlemen of the LSO put on their linen jackets, tug on their baggy Leeth Hill trousers and pat at pockets to be sure of the supply of cigarettes, pipe tobacco and pencils for the evening's crossword. Will Lang, the trumpet, and Donald Stewart, second violin, go off together in search of some inexpensive workers' café where they will, as always, sit side by side at adjoining tables like two blessed country vicars who have known what it is to toil in the midst of sin.

John Duffy, the personnel manager, comes bustling around, another long list in hand, looking this time for Gerry Newson, the number five double bass, 'my best pal'. For years, they were stand partners when John played in the orchestra. Over a half pint, one evening, they decided to go into business together and now command a team of ladies who sew double bass covers for them. 'We've sold three hundred all over Europe – and we don't even advertise, it's all word of mouth.' John has been back to America twice since the world tour: another business sideline, buying and selling stringed instruments. He has a holiday coming up next week: he is off with Claudio Abbado to the European Community Youth Orchestra. Nursing 150 young players through their grand tour is his idea of a rest. When he has a moment, he comes in, as now, with his eye darting about for his pal, someone to share things with. In the bleakest moments, they cheer one another up. John is separated; his work is his real life and it is all of it. Orchestras produce the kind of friendship, deep but usually unacknowledged, that the junior colonial service was famed for. Perhaps it is not dissimilar: they are all like-minded chaps doing their bit.

A small bunch of string players stick together: they are the freelances brought in to substitute or swell the ranks and to make no trouble. 'I'm only an extra' is their lonely call. One or two of them may be here by special invitation to try out, to see if they are the stuff that LSO members are made of. These 'possibles' are easy to spot as they hang around trying to look as if they have always belonged, hoping to be noticed and invited along for the evening by their overlords from the rank and file. The others, the regular extras whose living depends on being as acceptable as possible to as many as possible, do not push themselves forward. The older ones among them, those who have served their years in opera pits, have no wish to mingle anyway.

They have deliberately chosen the life of the extra for its independence. It is a matter of resentment that extras are looked down upon by orchestra members, patronized as if they are freelance by default, by reason of not being able to get a proper job. 'If only they asked me . . .,' one will say, 'I could tell them what's wrong around here.' And in the safe corners, around café tables where only other extras gather, they mutter treason against the LSO and talk of the joys of subbing for this or that other orchestra – as if they are any different wherever they play. They prize themselves on their detached and objective viewpoint. 'Don't be misled by looks,' they say ominously. 'You'd be surprised who you can hear and who you can't from where I sit.' And, such is the condition of being an extra stranded at the very back, that, in truth, they cannot hear themselves, let alone others.

One or two extras may be the young recognized talents of the moment, still at college perhaps, subbing for the experience and a bit of welcome income. They feel no restraint on their performance. They play every note, their bows and fingers go down purposefully on the strings: no tickling or faking for them. Since they are still accustomed to hearing themselves – mostly running through the solo repertoire in practice studios – they have enough confidence in their intonation to play out and trust that it is in tune. Such a performance does not, of course, show up the other players around in a very good light but it is not form to tell the latest big talent from the Royal Academy to ease off. 'What's that noise back there?' is a remark reserved only for the downtrodden extra, momentarily forgetting himself and producing more than his lowly position warrants.

The extras are the scullery maids, there to get on with it, eyes lowered, and not to interrupt their betters. Seen and not heard: the motto of the good extra. Only John Duffy understands them. He knows them all and has his private list of first-call players. He knows who are his rock-solid ticklers – the ones with no vibrato and limp wrists – who can, nevertheless, be relied upon for paying absolute attention. It is such a relief to have someone around who needs only be told something once. And then there are those who play as if in the preliminary of an international competition, as if to prove that an orchestra is not the death of individuality. These do not get invited back very often – is it John Duffy's mischievous way of giving the backstand members something of a shock to invite these sparklers at all? Surely not, for part of Duffy's skill is in knowing who will fit in but, more important, who will please a section. It is purgatory to sit next to a man who irritates: playing inflates everything out of proportion. The busy extra, therefore, is the one who can slip unnoticed into the ranks of the orchestra's faceless men.

Every orchestra has its quota of players who are so colourless that they can sit for years without being really known to all their colleagues. They are the ones who never warm up offstage for fear of being heard. They will, perhaps, take their seats a little early hoping to get in some discreet practising. If the stage is not yet noisy enough for them, they hold back, resorting for camouflage to fidgeting with music and pencils. As a last resort, they may pick up the instrument and work on it a bit using a mute. These orchestra mice usually keep themselves neat and tidy but let their instruments go uncared for: they change strings only when they break, there is always rosin dust everywhere.

Fortunately, they do not play strongly enough to break the bow hair so that it is less noticeable that their bows are hardly ever re-haired.

Just as there are some whose personalities defy description and whose names defy remembering, there are those characters known to everyone whose names, in time, become coupled with the orchestra as part of its identity. Everyone in the LSO, for instance, looks on Francis Saunders, the bespectacled cellist, as the orchestra's unofficial 'chaplain', unselfish, concerned and thoughtful: qualities, it should be said, that are not common in musicians, centred as they are around themselves and their instruments. Ashley Arbuckle, the co-leader, is taken to hospital in Salzburg with cysts on his throat. Francis goes to visit. Another cellist, Clive Gillinson, has twins who were born two months premature and spent weeks in the intensive care unit. Francis asks about them often and worries also about Clive's wife. 'It must be hard on her,' he says sympathetically. (As if life for an LSO wife was ever expected to be anything but hard.) When Francis is not playing, the section seems to be missing something. When both Francis and Clive are away, it seems bereft. It is a quality of the LSO that is sometimes overlooked: it puts a high value on niceness and decency.

According to orchestra lore, cellists and double basses are the most warm-hearted of sections. Is it something to do with the years spent hugging their instruments? Or do the big deep tones at the bottom attract more giving personalities? Cellists certainly look with wonder on violinists and the contortions that they must endure merely to hold a fiddle. What can it do to a man's psyche to spend a lifetime twisted in that unnatural fashion? Their special sympathy, however, is reserved for the second violins. These latter play almost entirely on the D and G strings which are on the far side of the instrument – they have to keep their bowing arm high above the shoulder merely to reach across to them. It is hard and tiring to play as a second and, at the end of it, it is for little seeming satisfaction. The firsts almost always have all the best tunes. But there are those who like to play second fiddle, with all that the name implies. They are hidden away and safe. Henry Greenwood, the librarian, used to play sub-principal in the seconds and turned down the chance to be 'promoted' to first. 'In the first violins you have to be a little bit crazy. They play the top line on the outside of the stage in front of 2000 people. Well, it would make my heart jump.'

Among the second violins, however, are several of the LSO's better-known characters. There is Terry Morton, a kind of upstanding LSO Ratty, hard-working, responsible and, currently, vice-chairman of the board. He shoulders his duties not with the wind player's bravura of Anthony Camden but with all the zealous attention of a good second violinist who sits up and plays every note of the music. And by way of contrast there is David Williams, a Welsh bear with a pirate's face and a reputation as the section's favoured 'bad boy'. The son of a butcher turned livestock dealer in Trefriw, he started music lessons late when he was 9. 'A man came to school and said "Do you want to learn the violin?" I didn't even know what a violin was but I fell in love with its gorgeous noise and beautiful shape.' Six months later, he was good enough to be playing on Llandudno Pier and it is that very facility that has hampered him. He never needed the discipline of practising regularly and for long hours – he just wanted to play. 'Basically, I was thick as two short planks, fairly shy and not very good at conversation so it was my way of talking and singing to masses of people.'

When he came to London to the Royal Academy, he remembers himself as 'a hunky Welsh mountain-type man' who still thought in Welsh, spoke English less well, and was obsessed with music. He must have been an exciting young player: he was only 23 when the LSO made him a member. But that was fourteen years ago. 'A lot of things you tend to accept – that you're not in the limelight, that you're part of a massive instrument but I'm afraid that I have become an automatic fiddle player. You fall into the pattern of the machinery.' The seconds play the harmonizing line to the first section, they provide the undercurrents, the other voice that speaks within. It may not require as much technique to play – the firsts play so often on the high strings where notes are closer together and need more dexterity to be accurate. But the seconds are often better orchestra musicians: they know how to listen, how to enhance others. Not for them the anarchy of seizing the melody and charging about with it.

But the boy of 9 who fell in love with the violin's singing tone did not dream then of being an 'inner voice'. David Williams often talks of *hiraeth*, the word in Welsh that means a longing to go back to where life started. It is the innocence of his feeling for music that he mourns. And yet, more than he sees, he still has it. It is one reason he smiles so much, why he is also liable to fret if he gets bored. 'I suppose', he says, fishing for another cigarette, 'it started as a way of covering up being a little worried and a little scared. I still sometimes feel sick before an important concert and, I mean, in the LSO it isn't nice to show it.'

Sunday morning
The Grosses Festspielhaus was built in 1959; the concert hall is coldly decorated in dark grey and black as if in repudiation of all the kitsch goings-on outside. It is only the second day in Salzburg but time seems to have stretched here. This morning's rehearsal is not going well: the concert tonight has produced the wrong kind of nerves. There is a way of being on edge that is the preliminary to excitement, but this is not it. The orchestra is too subdued, betraying uncertainty and a lack of confidence. Voices are too soft; everything is just a fraction self-conscious. The ease and flow of making music has seized up. Claudio Abbado, says LSO chairman Anthony Camden, is a bag of nerves. Anthony Camden is no better – he shows his own state by,

uncharacteristically, making trouble: it is already common knowledge that he reduced violinist Gillian Findlay to tears. Something about bare legs and shorts suddenly being inappropriate rehearsal wear.

A soloist, the Czech soprano Edita Gruberova, is warming up backstage before rehearsing two Mozart arias. Opera prima donnas are the last of the great stars. Outrageous and given to being difficult, they are for the most part thoroughly disliked by orchestra musicians. What an orchestra likes is to work with a singer who is a good trouper: Jessye Norman is a trouper, so too is Margaret Price. Madame Gruberova is an unknown quantity. It is worrying that she was called for 10 o'clock and that she has been striding up and down in her bare, harshly lit dressing room for over an hour. It is an encouraging sign, however, that she has not turned up with the singer's complement of groupies: a manager, a PR man, a husband and at least two wealthy patrons. It does not occur to Abbado that it is rude – or, at the very least, not especially flattering – to keep waiting one of the newest stars of the Vienna State Opera. It is simply that there is other music to rehearse.

Abbado probably does not even know that it is one of those notorious conductor's tricks to keep singers hanging around just to establish who is in charge. 'Being in charge' is not a Claudio preoccupation. Unlike some conductors, he enjoys working with a soloist. There is no feeling with him that he cannot wait for the other person's show to be over so that he can get on with his big symphony after the intermission. But he is not in the lonely hearts business: soloists who need love and reassurance from a conductor (and they are many) will be baffled by his reserve.

Edita Gruberova has a reputation as a dazzling virtuoso: her voice, they say, is technically capable of almost anything. As a result (and mostly, as is the way in music, on word of mouth) she is sought after by every major opera house in the world. She refuses almost every offer: the quality of her voice is rare enough to justify her wish for the highest fees, for only those roles that will show her off at her best, and her preference for singing only in prestigious new productions. An instrumental soloist's dream is to play after intermission in a concert that is being televised live and then sold to a videotape company. A prima donna wants to open the season with the music director himself in the pit and a new production that is untouched by another soprano. Concert arias are fillers by comparison, even when it is Salzburg.

Gruberova has never worked with either Abbado or the LSO: she came as part of the Festival package, acceptable and distinguished but a stranger, nevertheless. Who knows how she will react to such casual treatment? Or, more important still, what she will bring by way of inspiration to the LSO? A good soloist is like a good dinner guest, bringing more to the table than he or she takes away. The moment Edita Gruberova comes on stage, it is clear that she is one of the new, tough breed of women singers. This is no fragile little songbird: look in vain for the entourage or the protective male adorer to stand up for her. Her career is very much her own and she is here this morning to work. No perfumed gestures of greeting to the orchestra, no limpid looks at the conductor: she opens her music and gets ready to sing.

Truly, the voice is extraordinary. There is nothing to hide behind in Mozart, no drama or bits of theatrical business, only notes to be sung and the purest of music to bring to life. Peter Hemmings, the LSO managing director, an opera man through and through, sits in the stalls enthralled by the sheer perfection of her sound and by the breathtaking range that holds its volume and accuracy up to the highest imaginable notes. The orchestra is clearly impressed: no fuss *and* she sings in tune. An ideal, almost. But how interesting that Peter Hemmings, totally enthused, should have missed the danger sign. Is it true, perhaps, that no man can really understand this orchestra without playing in it?

There is in Gruberova's voice a hint of coldness: it is stunning but it does not have natural warmth. This does not detract from her performance – it is the intensity of passion not its colour that counts – but it will affect the LSO. You can hear it already in Anthony Camden's oboe. The first aria is almost a duet between singer and oboe. The steely technical tricks come naturally to Anthony; they are his forte as a player. It is in the softer, more vulnerable passages that he needs to be drawn. He can play with the gentlest and most touching line but he will, automatically, try first the other, easier way – better-dressed, less naked. He has to be inspired to draw on his deepest feeling although it is amazing that it is still there at all, given the hours he rushes around as chairman. A great oboe cannot play with armour around his soul.

Anthony will undoubtedly play beautifully tonight; with such an example before him, it will certainly be in tune (pitch being the oboe's constant obsession). It may not be magical, however. It is unfair because it is so terribly hard to play the oboe: all that pressure on the brain, minutes of playing without taking breath, the absurdity of depending on a miniscule piece of organic reed. And yet, more perhaps than any other instrument, the oboe must play magically. Claudio understands that: he hardly ever calls Anthony on a point or a phrase during rehearsals. He tries instead to reach him during concerts so that the shell can be set aside and the music within can come out. Letting go while being in complete control: that is all it takes. As if that was not everything.

For the moment, everyone pays lip service to how well it is going. Time for another Berlioz rehearsal: how many hundreds of hours by now has the LSO worked on this piece? Abbado's nervousness is coming through. Lowlier musicians often assume that someone of Abbado's stature is immune from nerves. When the symptoms start to show, they are misunderstood for wilful bloody-mindedness, as if Abbado could help himself any more than any other musician thrown off by a particular concert.

Robert Noble, *Leningrad*

Double Basses, Vienna

It is the bells upon which Abbado now focuses his restless energy. Bells are Abbado's special madness; all conductors have at least one. For the offstage church bells that sound during the devilish witches' sabbath, the LSO has had built a complicated, heavily amplified 'bedstead' on which have been stretched and wired six piano strings that are to bring bottom to the large chimes standing in its vicinity. This bedstead went to make its début on the world tour: some baggage handlers dropped it in Washington, it was repaired twice, blew in Philadelphia and could not be heard until, appropriately enough, the Japanese managed to put it into working order.

There are three percussionists involved with Berlioz's bells – at least the way that Claudio has them set up. There is one man on the bedstead, another on the chimes and yet a third on a pair of Burmese gongs. Most conductors give the cue, the bells strike and then the orchestra comes in around them. Not Claudio. The bells, according to Claudio, are never together. The bells, according to Claudio, are never loud enough. Or it is the wrong kind of loud. Thundering chimes peel offstage as the desperate percussionists, perched precariously on soap boxes, chairs, upturned shelves or whatever else might pass for the height of a steeple, hammer and blow and still Abbado's frenzied need to hear the ultimate bell sound goes unsatisfied.

A closed circuit TV camera has been rigged up so that the percussion can see Claudio's beating; what they see now is Claudio's furrowed brow as he sends the leader, Michael Davis, scampering around with the predictable message: 'More bells, sweetheart.' 'Bells, bells,' calls Abbado himself finally. 'Bells, are you there?' calls Mike. There are moments when being referred to as an instrument gets under the skin of the most easy-going of musicians. (Famous orchestra story: 'Clarinet, you're late,' calls a conductor. 'You hear that, you bugger?' the clarinettist addresses his stick. 'You're late.') Michael Frye, the principal percussion, is a hard man to rile: the LSO is smooth work next to the time he put in as drummer for pop star Mike Oldfield. Mike Frye stands back now, sniffs, shakes his long dark curls and gold jewellery, looks down and taps the bells knowingly: 'You're for it,' he tells the offenders before calling out with a certain irritation. 'The bells are here. Does he want to speak to them?' This irreverence is rewarded with the announcement that there will be a special bells rehearsal after the rest of the orchestra leaves at one o'clock.

It is quarter to two before Mike and his sub-principal, Ray Northcott, turn off the amplifier. Ray tidies up the full array of hammers with which he has been trying for a better bell: some with leather, some with felt, one with an old duster around the head. All in vain.

It might seem, to anyone but a percussion player that is, that tonight is Ray's big concert. The Webern is a star percussion piece. The fourth movement, which opens with an almost imperceptible side drum roll, is dominated by

Ray on the large orchestra gong: he seems to play alone, beating softly but obsessively. Offstage, the bells chime distantly. There should be a feeling otherwise of absolute and deathly silence, the only movements those of Claudio's baton and Ray's hammer. Quite a dramatic moment and entirely Ray's, rather a treat, you might think, for a man whose orchestra life is spent mostly being an anonymous banger and shaker of things in the loud parts.

That is to forget the notion of each instrument that every piece revolves around its own special contribution. Say 'the Eroica Symphony' to a horn player and he will immediately think in terms of the famous horn trio in the third movement that lasts all of a minute or two. Principal cellists are much given to talking of the slow movement of Brahms Second Piano Concerto as 'the cello movement' so that perhaps it serves them right to discover that clarinettists view Dvorák's cello concerto as a big clarinet piece. String players, as far as Ray Northcott is concerned, are mere toilers, playing every note and being heard in none. As second percussion, sub-principal, he sees himself as a man from whom each note counts. 'When you play percussion', he says with conviction, 'you take your life in your hands every time.' Bruckner's Eighth Symphony? Well over an hour of strenuous violin playing fades to muzak compared in his mind to the two crashing cymbal notes. 'They are very important – there would be a totally different climax without them.'

At least percussionists do not feel misunderstood; they have all those other ingenious percussionists around them. It is the infinite variety both of the noises themselves and the instruments on which they are produced that give them so much enjoyment. A dedicated percussion player will comb junk shops wherever he is in the hope of finding something unusual to take home and doctor. What else in the orchestra can come in with the impact of a good cymbal crash, saved as it is for the high point of the musical structure? 'People think you just pick up the cymbals and play them' – he sounds astonished. 'Do you know that an American has written a whole book on cymbal technique? Look at the alternatives: should it be a pair of cymbals or just one played with a stick? Should it be a hard stick or a soft stick? When I first joined this orchestra, there were so few percussion players in London you would even dare to give cymbals to, it was something to be discussed first.'

The string players may have their golden age of the Cremonese school of makers to look back on: percussion still has its sense of esoteric mystery. Zildian, the Stradivarius of cymbal making, continues to produce its great metal instruments, the secret for which has been kept in the male side of this Armenian family for generations. It was carried with it in flight from the massacres in Turkey to the safety of Boston, Mass., where it survives to this day. The LSO was the first London orchestra to use 24-inch cymbals, 6 inches bigger than the usual size, to get the deeper sound for Mahler. Its percussion section prides itself on its vast repertoire of things to beat ('the skill in playing any percussion instrument is not how you hit it but how you leave it'). Does any other symphony orchestra use tuned woodblocks or an ang-klung? This section, however, is part of an orchestra that was specially sought out by John Williams to record his scores for the *Star Wars* epics. In percussion terms that is the equivalent of a royal warrant.

The intergalactic strife of the Jedi may not be what Ray's father had in mind when he put him on the drum in his Salvation Army band. ('Never had a formal lesson in my life.') It is quite a way, too, from the RAF Central Band at Uxbridge in which he served for seven years (the LSO recruited him and then had to buy him out of his service contract). But compared to the challenge of finding the right beating surface to commemorate Hollywood's sci-fi beasts, this evening's Webern is fairly busy but no harder than usual. Nine notes on the glockenspiel, a little bit at the end with root twigs and the big solo with the large gong – which was bought specially for Claudio ('to satisfy his desire for depth'). It is nothing next to the aggravation of the offstage bells in the Berlioz. 'Webern is not difficult, it's important to get the pulse of the movement at the beginning that's all. There are two or three good beating spots in a gong and you have to find the nicest place for that particular piece. But it's only a few bars, so what's the fuss about? Personally, I don't think the Webern is worth that amount of thought.'

On his way out of the courtyard to treat himself to a greasy, overcooked omelet in a cheap café, Ray stops to absorb the warmth and brightness of the Salzburg afternoon. There is always this surprise after a rehearsal to find the world outside still in place. Through a window somewhere come the strains of another orchestra serving its time in the paint shop upstairs. The Berlin Philharmonic, perhaps? Or is it the Vienna? Ray, with the sensitivity of a man who once tuned pianos and cathedral organs, winces as the sound forces itself upon him. The timpani is sharp. The search for perfect pitch: it is the alchemy of today's orchestras.

Pitch, of course, is the first ground on which an unconvinced listener attacks an orchestra; or rather, imperfect pitch, to be exact. Is there a sense that something is not right? Put it down to bad intonation. Pitch is the most frustrating of musical fetishes for it is, in its perfect state, utterly unattainable. One hundred musicians all playing at once – it is unthinkable that they might all play exactly in tune with one another. It is one of the attractions of chamber music to the purist: it cuts down the odds against getting it right. Pitch is a variable: how far it can stray before it starts to sound sour is as much a reflection on a listener's own ear as on any absolute. British and American orchestras take the A at a frequency of 440 hertz; Austrian and German at 444. That the latter are spoken of not as sharp but as brilliant is a measure only of the degree to which they all play with exactly the same amount of sharpness. The LSO has a miserable time with pitch; what orchestra does not? Sometimes it seems to be a very silly life indeed.

Late Sunday evening

Tonight it was Webern, Mozart and Berlioz. The orchestra was tense and it showed up within the first bars. Soon after the opening of the Webern, a horn player, high on a steep riser at the back of the stage, dropped his mute. It fell with a crack from one step to another: there was a loud report as it reached the bottom. Abbado, to his credit, controlled every natural impulse: his head never turned. It was an act of real generosity. Imagine the horror of the horn player tonight; these are moments that haunt a musician for years. ('Oh, he won't think twice about it,' said Peter Hemmings afterwards, with a disarming lack of understanding. 'I don't think they really bother about that kind of thing, do you?') After another few minutes, another dreadful moment: a percussion player moving between instruments was caught on a squeaking board in a phrase so quiet that the sound of this wood creaking went right to the back of the hall. The percussionist froze: he was unable to move backwards or to go on, fearing that the slightest movement would set off the board again. The bars seemed to stretch endlessly before an explosion of orchestra sound released him. It was impossible not to be riveted by his predicament and drawn away from the unfolding of Webern's music. After the 1938 *Anschluss*, Webern's music was banned in Austria by the Nazis so it is fitting enough that it should be played now. The audience obviously felt no special responsibility to Webern's memory: they coughed and fidgeted with the same abandon as they did in New York.

Madame Gruberova came out resplendent in a red taffeta ball gown with huge puffed sleeves and plunging neckline, a white flower and gold chains at her throat. She was, with her skilled make-up and hair styling, every inch the gorgeous prima donna. The Mozart arias were, everyone said, quite wonderful: the high notes had everyone marvelling at such vocal acrobatics. No one, however, said anything about spines that were chilled or hearts that stopped. The audience applauded and swept out for its nightly intermission promenade. Success is largely a matter of degree: there is good and there is great. Backstage, around the cold drinks machine in the courtyard, the word went round that this was a great success by Salzburg standards. Stuffy audiences, it was decided, do not stamp and shout with appreciation. The Berlioz went well: it was both well played and well received. But this was the opening orchestral concert of the Festival: at the end of the month, how many will still remember and talk of it?

Deutsche Grammophon Production of Hamburg and Harold Holt Ltd of London have arranged a joint party after the concert at the Gasthof zum Hirschen at Parsch for Claudio Abbado and the LSO. Martin Campbell-White, a director of the Harold Holt agency, is Claudio's British manager. He is here for the Salzburg concerts. During the day he can be seen about town, briefcase in hand, on his way to hold significant conversations with DG and to hear the worst from the LSO. Martin once played the bassoon; he is still best understood from the point of view of that instrument's rather curious character.

The bassoon is the low voice of reason in the wind choir, always restrained, never hysterical, knowing just when to bring humour to a situation (Haydn's symphonies are full of pranks and jokes written for the bassoon). It is easy to overlook the bassoon's voice in an orchestra – generally, it lacks those ear-catching solo moments – but without its low register and firm rhythmic pulse, the wind section would have no body or direction. It knits together the different sonorities around it: it often holds a music theme steady while, in the upper octave, the line is tossed from oboe to flute to clarinet. It is the only reed instrument that blends immaculately with the horns – a key function in an orchestra.

This is not to say that the bassoon is a dull fellow: imagine a mediocre musician entrusted with the bassoon's opening statement in *The Rite of Spring*, an entrance to the primordial world that is to come. It may be the forgotten instrument among most audiences but sooner or later it makes its impact: who could ignore the bassoon's melancholy solo at the beginning of Tchaikovsky's *Pathétique Symphony*? In the hands of a good bassoonist, it can set the mood for the whole symphony to come. Thus Martin Campbell-White knits together and underpins the conflicting interests and desires of Claudio Abbado, the LSO, Deutsche Grammophon and anyone else who counts, while his bassoonist's chuckle has defused many an awkward moment around a lunch table.

Agents have a delicate relationship with artists. They must believe in them, befriend them and yet not forget that without them there would be no income. No one client can, or should, provide even a lion's share of what is needed to run a management office. And yet no major artist is ever prepared to admit that there is a rival for the manager's affection – or at least for his time. No one wants to hear of an agent's commitment to others.

Twenty artists or sixty (Martin represents thirty-one) and each one, despite all denials, wants the illusion of believing himself to be the most important and held the most dear. Martin represents other conductors, Simon Rattle and Andrew Davis included, but tonight he belongs entirely to Claudio. This party is his way of expressing that but, good bassoonist that he is, he steps back discreetly and allows his co-hosts, the terriers from Polydor, to bustle about, placing guests at the table and being sure to flank Claudio with Deutsche Grammophon directors. From the far end of the table, Martin keeps a weather watch.

It is still too soon after the concert for anyone to talk of it normally or dispassionately. Conversation is general, skittering around international music gossip (who will replace Giulini in Los Angeles? Why has Anthony Bliss really left the Metropolitan Opera house in New York? If Muti gets Berlin, what will happen to Philadelphia?), the lovely summer days, the overcrowding at the Goldener Hirsch and various dinners eaten in Europe this summer. The unwitting silence about the concert is in itself a verdict on it. Had it been disastrous, or even troubled, it would be impossible to avoid the subject. Everyone concerned would be slightly uncomfortable and tense. Conversation would jump around, settling nowhere, starting and stopping suddenly. There would, too, be more tired-looking faces: nothing is as draining as being involved in a bad concert. Had it been a truly exciting event, on the other hand, everyone would be bubbling over with it. That horn entrance, the way the violins played the waltz: everyone has his own particular moment from a terrific performance. The 'high' becomes tangible. People hug and touch more, smile without being aware of it. Everything, in short, becomes physically much looser. This party, gathered in the private room of an elegant Italian restaurant, flows smoothly. There has been a concert; it was good, it was very good but that is not enough.

7: Second Chances

Monday morning

It is 90° outside, close and heavy. In the paint shop of the Festspielhaus, the fumes from various tins left open overnight have become so strong that visitors arrive and as quickly leave. The orchestra, however, is trapped here for six hours today rehearsing for the second concert. Ah well, the suggestion goes, worse things happen. It is unbearably hot and it smells ghastly. The silent Festspielhaus official takes to closing all the windows every now and again – the noise of the traffic clearly bothers him – so that Anthony Camden and Mike Davis have to run around after him opening them all between solos. And still there is a surprisingly jolly note in the air. Last night is over; the orchestra has forgotten its unease. The players have convinced themselves that the concert was splendid and rapturously received – easy enough to do when it actually went quite well – and some of the confidence and swagger has returned. It was a near thing; they pulled it off. Every musician knows that feeling of reprieve after getting by a great deal less disastrously than was feared. What might have been acquires a life of its own in retrospect: euphoria sets in.

The morning is spent rehearsing *Pictures at an Exhibition*. Happily, there are not many hidden traps in it. The orchestra has been through the trial of fire with this piece: they recorded it for Deutsche Grammophon with Abbado not long ago. Some musicians thrive in a studio; not Claudio. Like many old-time musicians, Toscanini for one, he needs the inspiration of performing to an audience. He can neither turn it on instantly for the microphones nor overlook the details over which he fusses so in rehearsals. To have recorded a difficult virtuoso piece such as this, to have concentrated on it intensely for many hours, troubling over each phrase in the playback afterwards – all this brings to the LSO a confident belief that a concert performance of it is child's play now.

There are pieces that are tremendously taxing without the effort being in the least discernible to an audience, unless there is a real mess. Schubert's Ninth Symphony is written in such a way that if it is played well, it seems to float of its own accord without any visible striving. Meanwhile, in reality it is excruciatingly hard just to get through it. It needs delicacy, control and stamina of such an order that somewhere in the LSO library, an unknown

Anthony Chidell, *Carnegie Hall, New York*

soldier in the first violins has written in large pencilled letters a note of encouragement lest he give up: 'Only two pages to go'. And out there in the concert hall as the Ninth draws to a close, most people are completely unaware of arms dropping with fatigue, fingers aching and string players gasping for breath. *Pictures* is different, like being in the circus: every trick is announced and highlighted by Ravel's uncanny and brilliant orchestration. A rest before each such solo, a chance to recover afterwards. It is a true relief for the LSO. Every soloist and every section has its chance to shine and no one need be inhibited by a quest for subtle meaning.

If it is anybody's piece, it is the trumpet's. His solo opens the first of the promenades, supposedly a personification of Mussorgsky himself as he walks round the exhibition. A little later, the muted trumpet portrays Schmuyle, the poor Jew, bleating with self-pity. Maurice Murphy, the principal trumpet, is one of the LSO's favourites. It takes a while to realize how much he means to his colleagues; the LSO is such a boisterous crew that it is easy not to notice how undemonstrative it is at the same time. The clue is the way musicians listen: in rehearsals, and especially in concerts, they really listen when Maurice plays. They stop fidgeting, talking, daydreaming and all the other things musicians resort to in order to while away the time when they are no longer involved in the music.

Pictures is a feast of instrumental colour. Long before it is his solo, Duggie Cummings can be heard ripping into the first seven notes played by the cello section as it describes a small, twisted toy gnome. He has been principal cello of the LSO for sixteen years and he can still greet a meaty phrase with exuberance and enthusiasm. It is interesting that Claudio has his least complicated relationship of all the LSO principals with Duggie. The one so quiet and fastidious, the other so wild and extravagant but, as so often happens in music, two seemingly contradictory figures who share the same musical outlook. Claudio and Duggie still have an intense delight in music even after they have played it time and again over the years. It is a gift; musicians are often accused of being spoiled or of growing jaded when all that has happened is that they have grown older.

There are ten pictures in the exhibition and each one has its individual instrumental feature. Jack Brymer on saxophone recalls the soulful troubadour beneath The Old Castle. Dennis Wick, principal trombone in fact, plays one of the most famous of tuba solos – Bydlo. John Fletcher, the principal tuba, turns away from this chance of a moment in the spotlight for the satisfaction of the big blow, usually fortissimo, going on and on. ('If you're a bottom man,' he says, 'there are many ways of being on the bottom.') The tuba in full flight is like a storm at sea: one man doing all that can get pretty carried away. The Great Gate of Kiev, the last picture, is a huge battery of sound with gongs, bells, snarling trombones and growling tuba and everyone onstage at top volume. It feels good to let rip sometimes.

Eric Crees and Denis Wick, *Edinburgh*

Maurice Murphy, *Henry Wood Hall, London*

Monday afternoon

The morning went well and the afternoon promises well, too: the Brahms First Piano Concerto with Vladimir Ashkenazy, an old friend. The piano is about every concert goer's favourite solo instrument, if only for its repertoire: the Emperor, Tchaikovsky One, Brahms Two, Mendelssohn at his most lyrical and reams of glorious Mozart. It is the one instrument that can make itself heard above a full symphony orchestra without relying too much on that orchestra's consideration. Maybe four or five times as many pianists appear with the LSO in a year as all the other solo instrumentalists together. And yet very few pianists can really inspire an orchestra with their playing. It is essentially a percussive instrument – interpreted literally, all too often, as something to be banged. It does not have, naturally, that sustained, singing tone to which musicians most readily respond. The piano is perforce set apart from an orchestra by size, appearance, position, sound and attack. It is indeed the stranger in the family. Who, except for the orchestra pianist hidden away backstage somewhere, can identify with the heroic figure seated out there at his black box? To string players a violinist is one of 'us', his success is 'ours'. A pianist is an outsider, no kith and kin of his here.

Many pianists rub home this estrangement; they come out and bang the A with about as much sensitivity as a hammer. It gets the orchestra's attention – as is intended – but hardly wins its sympathy. The piano is the one instrument that is totally self-sufficient. It has enough music for a lifetime of playing alone without ever needing another musician. A pianist, in his developing years, practises alone in a room for hours on end. Other instruments have to learn to get along musically with one another as part of mastering their technique; pianists are loners from the very beginning.

Vladimir 'Vova' Ashkenazy bounces out of the lift into the paint shop and at once a beam spreads across his expressive Russian face. He is, says that beam, happy to be with his friends again. Delighted, in fact. Soloists make many varieties of entrance into a first rehearsal, most of them to do with an awareness of being looked at and an assumption that they will be paid attention to. Some bow and scrape seeking approval; others sail in looking for deference. Most of them have what might be termed a royalty complex: however nice they are, however unassuming, they tend to believe deep down that they are called to higher things than other mortals. They seek both reassurance and re-engagement from musicians who may earn ten times less than they. Vova Ashkenazy makes no such entrance and the contrast with others is immediate – but then he has worked with the LSO for almost twenty years. He is a man who has left behind his country – he lives in Switzerland now – so the musicians he knows and trusts have become the countrymen of his later life.

As he walks over to the piano, a great cheer goes round the LSO. He turns and waves his arms above his head like a prize-fighting elf. It is extraordinary

Jennifer Brown, *Barbican, London*

to see how the orchestra snaps suddenly awake; the adrenalin is almost visible as it starts to flow. Most soloists are takers; very few have this confidence to be givers as well. Ashkenazy, along with Alfred Brendel, Maurizio Pollini and Rudolf Serkin, is on Claudio's list of number one-approved pianists. The four are very different musicians: all that they have in common is their instrument. Brendel, the thoughtful intellectual; Pollini, the austere technician; Serkin, the wise guru; and now Ashkenazy, the bewitching life force. He and Abbado have not even bothered to get together in a private run-through before this orchestra rehearsal; they feel no need. They are what musicians call 'a good fit'.

The paint fumes are dreadful. Jenny Brown, the gentle and stalwart cellist from the second desk, passed out this morning; she played on until the last second. Her father, Jim Brown, is having to share the burden of first horn for the time being as David Cripps unexpectedly left that seat free when he sailed off to New Zealand last week with his new second wife (formerly the managing director's secretary). LSO marital sagas are usually expected to take second place to the orchestra; clearly, this one got out of hand. Jim Brown is standing in. He is one of those steady veterans who never let the side down. He has seen service, as London musicians do, in many orchestras: the Scottish National, Royal Opera House, London Philharmonic, Philharmonia, Royal Philharmonic, National Philharmonic and now the LSO.

James Brown sat in the heat this morning playing all those taxing solos in *Pictures from an Exhibition*. And with each one his daughter, Jenny, grew more anxious. Her father had one heart attack long ago, he is overweight and surely not meant to be playing demanding solos in these conditions. Jim Brown is in fine fettle; it was Jenny who, to her shame, fainted silently away. There are only two women members of the LSO and they are still something of a novelty. Gillian Findlay, the outspoken first violinist, joined in 1980 and Jenny followed her two years later. Gillian seems the more extrovert, 'one of the boys'. Jenny, outwardly, is a Jane Austen-ish figure, a gentle heroine who nevertheless endures with singular loyalty. No one who is an entirely delicate-heroine type sits number three in the LSO cello section. It takes strength to turn up day after day and last the LSO's long hours; the instrument itself needs muscle and grit. It was to be expected that if Jenny had to faint she would do so gracefully and without interrupting her stand partner.

But despite the fumes and heat, the orchestra is playing wonderfully. Vova now conducts as well as plays; the Philharmonia is his natural home ('I will be a pianist for the LSO but not a conductor,' he has said). The LSO somehow missed the signs and it was the Philharmonia who gave Ashkenazy the chance to work on this broader musical canvas. It means that he is one of the few pianists who really notices individual musicians in the orchestra, responds to and blends in with them and allows the orchestra to have the lead if the music is written that way. He has long since overcome the pianist's automatic obsession with his own part, with just playing as many of the written notes as is humanly possible. That he misses almost nothing is something that audiences might not catch. (A pianist has so many notes, what difference does one or two more or less make in the end?) It impresses orchestra musicians, however; they are too used to those who fake and muddy their way through the odd terrifying moment when hands are flying everywhere at once. Ashkenazy is short and he moves briskly, which makes him seem slighter than he is. His upper arms and shoulders have enormous strength. Critics pay tribute to his 'resonant tone' but, put more simply, he can make an extraordinary amount of noise on the piano. He can also produce soft, slow moments that are very fragile. Brahms's First Piano Concerto was originally intended to be a symphony and it has the strength of symphonic writing in the orchestra part. The LSO plays out to Ashkenazy. At the end of the rehearsal, there is another rousing cheer. Why can it not always be like this?

Monday evening

On the ramparts of the medieval fortress that towers above Salzburg there is an outdoor café much frequented by tourists. The tables by the wall are reserved for those who order food as well as drinks. There has been some discussion between the sharp-faced waitress and Douglas Cummings concerning his having taken possession of a prized wall-side table with the intention only of drinking there. Duggie, ever one for the large gesture, offers to order the most expensive item on the menu. More conservative counsel prevails which results in Duggie and his companions, Jenny Brown and John Fletcher, he of the tuba, retiring to a centre table under a large, old tree for a glass of wine. Hardly another soul has braved the ride up the funicular, for black clouds hang over the mountains: a storm has been forecast.

Rumour has it that John has resigned from the LSO, something to do with not being given time off by the release committee to play a date with the Philip Jones Brass Ensemble and, furthermore, being left with the impression that soloists are not expected to carry on as if deserving of special consideration. Duggie, Jenny and John are comrades of the bass clef. Those who play the bass line are natural allies, sticking together. They share all the same problems of clarity, of having to be strict and firm at the bottom and yet always flexible, and also the unvoiced envy of the violins running around up high with the best tunes. ('Violins? Ah, you can't deny the chihuahua his moment', says John.)

Tonight is a free night before tomorrow's concert and the cellists are bent on wooing John back into the fold. They need his fierce and uncompromising personality: he is the LSO's old thunderer, shaking his fist at the wayward habits of those among whom he finds himself. It is not his age – he is only 42. It is partly a reflection of his upbringing: 'My father was a schoolteacher and he had certain fanatical beliefs about what music was for that I have inherited.' It is also something to do with the nature of the instrument he plays; grunting, tough, the orchestra's guardian of outrage and anger.

Over a drink Duggie, with all the lyrical charm native to a cello, tries to win round this bearded and angular prophet. A thousand of their musical dialogues have sounded like this. The tuba, so large that the player sometimes seems to be skulking within, snarls its words of warning and vision of doom. It is only children who still fondly picture Tubby the Tuba. (In America, this famous musical portrait has been attacked by tuba players as inflammatory, so much so that they say it should never be performed.) No, John finally admits, it was not just his run-in with the release committee. That was the last straw. Years of living with compromises within the LSO have led to this.

While they have been talking, the sky has grown black and a huge wind blows across the outdoor terrace. This terrace is suddenly so battered by gusts that it starts to lose all its furnishings. Red-and-white checked table-cloths sail high over the wall and disappear. Glasses and bottles dance across the floor, until they shatter against the stones. A chair flies away in a particularly vicious moment. And as the noise of this drama mounts, John Fletcher's voice rises above it to the heavens. 'Music is not merely a commodity for entertainment', he declaims on this storm-racked pinnacle above Salzburg. 'And the music industry must not ignore the betterment of man's mental and spiritual state.' Art, religion and music: John Fletcher's trinity. Who can be surprised that the LSO with its regular bookings of light sessions and anything-for-money recordings has finally so undermined this purist that he sees himself as having given way, colluded with the abasement of all his beliefs? The LSO, he calls out through the sheets of rain, is no better than it should be. In this most Shakespearean of settings, he is another Lear railing against the gods – or at least against the standards of certain of his colleagues in the LSO.

Once, in an ideal time, when this fortress was first built, music served the church which took into its employ serious men of purpose. By the time Mozart was alive, it had become music's aim to serve and to please the noblemen of Europe who were at least educated in the art of listening attentively. In retrospect, that was a golden age. ('Of course, a lot of them talked through it and didn't care a sod,' John concedes during this discourse to the elements.) His lament continues. 'The world of music we live in was something that was liberated by Beethoven – by his expressive vocabulary, by the concept of the big concert, not of an evening's event in a castle. But to realize its very grandest functions requires education in the music vocabulary. We've left it too late, too late.' Music as a scenario for argument and conviction or music as a series of well-paid sessions for those who play it? Is Webern a tiresome composer whose music should not be put in programmes because it keeps audiences away or, as John will have it on this stormy night, the greatest leap forward since the Eroica Symphony?

Jenny and Duggie slowly coax him away from the ramparts, from the stunning spectacle of lightning and thunder swirling around their heads. The party is eventually installed inside the fortress's cosy restaurant. The odd chair and tablecloth continue to fly past the window by their table; it will be hours before the storm moves on and it is safe to come out. A large pepper steak, a good red wine and John both dries out and cheers up. Later, as the three walk down the steep, serpentine path back into town, John's one concern is that he has promised his young goddaughter that she should hear him play the Berlioz *Symphonie Fantastique* at the Proms this summer. 'That hurts most of all,' he says in a doleful voice, 'but I've made up my mind. Tomorrow is my last concert and then goodbye.' So tomorrow night's *Pictures* will be his very last LSO blow, perhaps for ever. Duggie Cummings refuses to believe it. Finally, on hearing how many hours Anthony Camden has spent trying in vain to give back his resignation to John, Duggie admits that the unthinkable can happen. 'I can't bear it,' he bursts out at one point. 'We need you. I need you.' The cold, cruel truth is that an orchestra depends on no man.

'I do feel something about the orchestra that is terribly important to me', Anthony Camden says at one point. 'There is the London Symphony Orchestra and no one individual player in any shape or form is bigger than that.' He knows exactly what he is saying. One of the most awesome sights in the LSO, for those who know and who remember what happened, is that of the oboist Roger Lord sitting at the end of the section. He never seems to say a word. His long, thin face is always still, staring either straight in front or straight down. With his long white hair, huge domed forehead and that far-away stillness, there is something heroic about him. Roger Lord was among the greatest of all oboe players; he could spin a phrase with that spellbinding beauty that is the gift of few. From joining the orchestra in 1952 until the late 1960s, he was as principal oboe, the true soul of the LSO. Impossible then to imagine the orchestra without his special voice. But muscles weaken and pressure takes its toll. When his wife, the composer Madeleine Dring, died suddenly, it was as if everything was finally too much for him. Anthony Camden moved from cor anglais and subsequently in to the first chair.

It was in Salzburg in 1976 that Roger had one of those friendly lunches between colleagues, with a member of the LSO board. He never played regular first again and has, seemingly, never wanted to. He is now the oboe's infantryman, there to swell the sound, not to lead it. Sometimes, though, in a particularly touching moment when Anthony is playing at his most giving, Roger Lord cannot help but give the slightest nod. It reaches him; the knot can never be entirely severed. A younger musician, who knew his playing only through recordings, went up to him a while ago just out of a desire to shake his hand: 'I wish I had heard you play the Eroica,' he said by way of expressing his admiration. 'You can't mean me,' said Roger Lord, looking both astonished and upset. 'I think you must have the wrong person.'

Tuesday afternoon

The Hotel Stein-Lecher is on the outskirts of Salzburg. In the garden, is a party: lots of babies, young fathers with small moustaches, a table of pretty young women and, around them, the arms of many smiling grandmotherly types. Along the hedge, a trestle table is laid out with champagne, orange juice and large platters of salami and ham sandwiches. Loaded on chairs under the trees are heaps of gift-wrapped offerings. Russell Jordan, an LSO percussionist and possessor of one of the smoothest of timpani rolls, was married this morning in the Marmorsaal of the Mirabell Palace. This afternoon is his wedding tea and by eight he must be in the Festspielhaus ready to play *Pictures* on the second half of tonight's concert.

His wedding was sandwiched into the rehearsal so that he had to rush back to play straight after the ceremony. There his bride was lured on stage by the crafty Anthony Camden who placed her under the grim Festspielhaus spotlights, blushing, giggling and thrilled, while the LSO played a spirited wedding march for her. It was very corny and everyone loved it. Nothing shows up how accustomed the orchestra gets to being tired, overworked and middle-aged as its sentimental delight in a full-blown romantic wedding: satin dress, flowers, shining eyes and all. Russell Jordan's wedding is a happy and private moment for the LSO – and to be savoured. For once, something takes precedence over whether the concert comes off and whether the latest financial problem can be overcome. Russell, with his hair slicked down, looking young and dandy in his grey slub suit and new silk tie, is going to have a wonderful wedding day. He is utterly pleased with himself and with life. Who could not respond? The whole orchestra has been invited to celebrate with him at the Hotel Stein-Lecher. It is interesting to see who comes. Maurice Murphy, for one. He has to play *Pictures* in a few hours but it is a question of priorities for him. He might prefer to be back at his hotel, taking it easy and getting ready for his big night but, in his book, a man does not miss a 'family' wedding for specious reasons like that. All the percussion are here bustling about in their best suits: Russell is their very own boy. Francis, from the cello section, comes bearing a present. There is a double bass or two, another cellist. Is it coincidence that the violinists have not turned up, not even the leader, Mike Davis? Every family has its members who put in the work to keep it together; in an orchestra, so often they are the brass and the men on the bottom. Sue Mallet has made the effort to come; she would. She alway does. She is due for yet another meeting at the Festspielhaus so she balances her glass with her 'nosebag', a big leather portmanteau in which she keeps her 'brains': a present from the LSO after the American tour, and she is secretly very proud of it.

Roger Lord, *Henry Wood Hall, London*

When a few large drops of rain begin to fall through rustling trees, everyone smiles more and picks up whatever is handy to carry into the hotel: babies, presents, bottles, chairs. By the time the party has crowded out the small lobby, the rain is torrential. Another Salzburg summer storm. Deep puddles and rushing rivers soon cover the road; the traffic is at a standstill queueing into town. There is not a taxi to be had. Some of the musicians, worrying about the 7.30 downbeat, decide to walk back. Within seconds they can be seen, drenched and bedraggled, sloshing through the water. Some scrounge lifts, some steel their nerves to wait it out. Nevertheless, by the time the London Symphony Orchestra walks out together on to the stage of the Festspielhaus, every member is in place even if some wet heads still shine brilliantly beneath the lights.

It is still pouring, the streets are clogged with cars and pedestrians pick their way in evening shoes around the pavement ponds. This is Salzburg; the concert must start on time. The Brahms Piano Concerto No. 1 will not wait. Soloists, as a rule, do not like to open a concert. Closing a concert, they realize, is a distinction given to very few: James Galway, perhaps, and any pianist over 80. Opening a concert is hard: it means coming out cold, with nothing to warm up the audience. There is the inevitable interruption to the music's flow after the first movement when latecomers stream in and cannot find the place in their programmes. Those who were on time are still thinking of other things: their income tax, the phone call they forgot to make, the headache that settled in at five. A sprightly overture would charm away such distractions.

Vladimir Ashkenazy does not seem to mind a jot; he bounds out with Abbado at his heels, sits down and gives the signal that he is ready. He is the least fussy of pianists: no fretting about the piano stool, no fidgeting with his shirt cuffs, no examining his fingers as if seeing them for the first time, no grimaces, no singing along as he plays. Tomorrow Edward Greenfield in the *Guardian* will pay tribute: 'Keyboard Titan . . . heroic poetry . . . seemingly telescopic fingers . . . phenomenal'. Tonight, the audience responds more directly: it stands up and it cheers. So much for the stuffed shirts who are said to clap in velvet gloves: it is the loudest and warmest of receptions. And the effect lingers. *Pictures at an Exhibition* is, when all is said and done, a marvellous piece of entertainment. The audience may be impressed by Lorin Maazel's weighty Bruckner next week; it simply delights tonight in the attractions of this old warhorse played with conviction. Another standing ovation for *Pictures*.

At a party given for Claudio after the concert at the Hotel Schloss Fuschl the atmosphere has a heady feeling. After such a night, anything is possible. Over the avocado with fresh lobster salad, there is talk of next spring's Beethoven cycle with Pollini playing the five piano concerti. Over the rolled fillet of veal on morels, there is talk of the Second Viennese School festival coming up, Berg and Webern in London, Paris and Vienna. Over the iced soufflé glacé Grand Marnier, there is talk of a huge Mahler festival in London, 1985. Over the black coffee, Jack Maxwell, formerly of United Drapery Stores, LSO old friend and patron, remarks that the orchestra has never been in such terrible financial shape. It seems an inappropriate thought.

On Wednesday morning at 9.30, the LSO checks in for the flight home to London. Salzburg, music at its most luxurious, is over. There are four pop concerts with Henry 'Moon River' Mancini to look forward to and, it is to be hoped, doses of well-paid light music recordings. At other gates, other Salzburg folk leave for a few days in the south of France, a quick trip to villas in Sardinia, a week with friends on Greek islands. The summer of the rich lasts a long time. It is a tantalizing glimpse of another life.

8: The New Young Crop

London, a few weeks later

There is a condition that John Fletcher, that prophet of the tuba, likes to refer to as 'dustbowl farming', the forcing and exploiting of young talent too early. He issues dire warnings about what will become of music if it continues to devour its young instead of protecting them. There is no anonymity within the music world: out of that crowd of black-and-white garbed musicians on stage, it is always known who is carrying the hopes of the future, being given opportunities to play too much, too quickly. Few can continue to grow under the pressure and fewer keep the motivation to do so. Being gifted is a passive condition, thought to last for ever, whereas all too often the seam of natural talent is quickly worked out. What could be a long and satisfying career peaks within a few years, leaving ahead a lifetime of pedestrian playing, of boredom and bitterness. This is John Fletcher's 'dustbowl farming, the greatest crime in music'. Facility and imagination are part of what makes a musician: study, curiosity, experience, discipline, also have their place. 'We must look after the earth and feed things into it,' as John says.

The European Community Youth Orchestra, music director Claudio Abbado, is, at least on the surface, an attempt to remedy that condition. Every summer, the finest young musicians in Europe come together by a strict auditioning system to study, rehearse and tour. Last year there was a month's retreat in Courchevel, with mountains, pastures, Mahleresque cowbells; this year it was Sicily, Taormina and Mount Etna. This is the 'A' circuit with concerts afterwards in Vienna, Amsterdam, Salzburg and Paris and on the podium conductors such as Solti, von Karajan and Abbado himself. The major orchestra principals come to coach: the violist Daniel Benyamini from the Israel Philharmonic, winds and strings from Chicago and, of course, a special contingent from the London Symphony Orchestra. It is exalted stuff. This is Claudio's training orchestra. It is on these young musicians that he will have his greatest impact: 'Claudio's virgins', unspoiled and unsullied. Their presence and enthusiasm arouses somewhat mixed feelings among those who have to earn their daily bread playing Mahler not for the first but for the two hundredth time.

The LSO is well aware of the imminent arrival in London of this year's European Community Youth Orchestra – coming to make its début at the Proms in the Albert Hall. The programme has its share of familiar Claudio

Ray Northcott and Michael Frye, *Salisbury Cathedral*

repertoire: the Webern Six Pieces for Orchestra, Op. 6, the Strauss *Tod und Verklärung* (Death and Transfiguration), another emotional wringer. The concert is the last of this year's ECYO tour.

On Monday morning, the orchestra gathers in the Albert Hall to rehearse. Ticket sales for tonight are poor but it is far from a jolly evening with all those heavy musical puddings: Wagner, Schumann, Strauss and Webern. Outsiders may point to the box office as confirmation that this is not much of an event. The presence of so many onlookers and visitors inside the hall during the rehearsal disproves that. It underlines the perpetual contradiction of classical music that art and accounting are not necessarily compatible.

Around the hall, there are clusters of musicians here to visit, to greet and to catch up. If this is the best, they want to hear it. The LSO, too, has its representatives. Most significantly, Anthony Camden sits in a front row rummaging through his copious Gladstone bag full of official papers, every inch the senior statesman. After Salzburg, he went with Claudio to join the ECYO and to coach the wind section. It did not go down well with everyone when he arrived and set to shuffling players around. He was none too pleased to find that even in this most idealistic of orchestras some players were sitting first solely by virtue of being one year older. How quickly the tradition of Buggins's turn sets into orchestra life as if it is an inevitable blight!

No wonder Anthony 'The Whizzer' Camden is busying himself with his papers in such a serious and weighty fashion. With the best will in the world, it is hard for grown-ups to cope with all the rampaging energy of youth set down in the ECYO. The principal oboe, a very beautiful player, is one of Anthony's long-time students. How complex his reaction must be as musicians come over to him with compliments about her phrasing and her pure sound. He must feel proud but is there also a twinge of regret, perhaps? Or at least of nostalgia for a simpler age when everything was new and fresh, as it is now for her?

The differences between this and an older professional orchestra stand out at once. Some are unexpected: there are more backstand slouches than in the London Symphony. They can get away with it here because they are young and good-looking; it takes a while to see past appearances, to notice the bowing arms that lack enough tension, the head crescendos in which tossing hair replaces making more sound. Alas, there are those who know that they have been judged and dismissed, excluded from the charmed circle of the front desks. Few at this age have much concept of working for themselves: their effort has always been directed by and for the approval of their olders and betters. Many is the 14-year-old Heifetz who levels out and finds himself ordinary again at 20. It is hard not to feel the waning interest from others. The ECYO has its share of those who know deep down that once they had brilliant potential.

There are enough others who abound with the vitality that marks the very talented when they are still utterly sure of themselves. It is revealed in the giggling and the snorts of laughter, the waving to friends and colleagues, the sense of being someone to admire, the bandroom serenading. ('All blowing away beforehand,' grumbles a coach. 'They're worn out by the time they go on stage.') Before the rehearsal there are snatches of the more lyrical violin concertos, Tchaikovsky and Beethoven for preference. A horn player somewhere has been 'practising his licks', running over a hard spot again and again. 'Oh Christ, I hope he gets it right when it matters,' says the coach wearily.

When Abbado calls the rehearsal to order, it is interesting to see how much younger he seems. In front of this orchestra he can drop his guard: its musicians sit before him grateful to be here. It is easier to be in love with playing music at this young age – naturally Abbado is at his best. When first they come to play for him, they have not the slightest idea about the vulgar gargoyles of Strauss tone paintings, about style, history or even good taste. What they have instead are clean slates. They do not know how to do it but they react quickly to such strong music and whatever happens, it is genuine. Abbado works with the ECYO for nine, ten, twelve hours a day until the music consumes them all. It is balm to his soul. No professional orchestra could do that for him. This dedication is an ideal to which every musician pays lip service. In truth, it can exist only in short, frenzied bursts among the very young. Such passion would not survive one year of playing LSO light session work for a fixer in North London.

After the ECYO concert, a crowd gathers round the stairway leading down to the underground dressing rooms. One of those Albert Hall specials, an old and bossy guard who has been here for ever, blocks the door to everyone. Those waiting are thus locked out and stranded anonymously in the corridor. The encore, Capulets and Montagues from Prokofiev's *Romeo and Juliet*, has left many flushed and laughing. It was played with swaggering bravura by 138 musicians who at that moment understood everything about being the great and proud young lords at court. At the doorway, waiting for a glimpse of them, stand those who were part of all this last year and are now too old or committed elsewhere. How insignificant they look next to the young stars of the evening who come bursting through the swing doors eager to be off to the big farewell party in the Serpentine Restaurant. Behind them stand the Mums and Dads. ('Go along darling, I know you want to be with your friends.') They pretend bravely to understand that they must be left behind this way. It is so often their dreams that are played out on stage. What child ever practised without a believer in the background?

The boys in their best suits, the girls in their Laura Ashleys: for some this will have been the highlight of their musical careers. If they are lucky, they do not yet understand that.

Tomorrow they scatter across the ten countries of the Common Market.

For one or two, it will be another work day. *Lohengrin* with Abbado and the LSO: angels, visions, effulgent glory and the Holy Grail.

At the end of the farewell ECYO party there is a cabaret, an impromptu affair, featuring the more extroverted of the orchestra's stars. In the thick of it, as always, is Wissam Boustany – wiggling, squealing, pouting, camping it up, anything for a laugh. Surrounded by all the understated English wind players present, it is hard to see in this outrageous flautist the product of several years at those worthy Manchester institutions, Chetham's School and the Royal Northern College of Music. 'He's marvellous, of course,' says Anthony Camden, 'but he's wild. 'You want to say, "Hey, hold on a bit."''

Wissam Boustany, first flute of the ECYO and guest second flute of the London Symphony Orchestra for the next few weeks, is 23 years old. On his wrist is a gold bracelet on which he has had engraved:'When I die may my body perish for it hinders me.' It was an eighteenth birthday present from his mother and stepfather. His stepfather is dead now. His mother is at home in east Beirut.

He carries with him a photograph of his stepfather: a wise and cultured-looking man, a pupil of the great New York violin teacher, Ivan Galamian, a follower of the Syrian poet and philosopher, Kahlil Gibran. 'My life, my real, my inspired life', says Wissam, 'started when my mother brought my step-father into our home. He brought me to music and taught me the value of loving something.' He is part Palestinian, part Lebanese, Christian on paper in a land where such things define life and death: of course he stands out as wild in the safe middle-class milieu of classical music. Before he stepped back and withdrew behind a façade of high spirits, he used to try to explain something of Beirut to colleagues who asked: 'I'd say people die there, are raped, throats cut, bodies are dumped near garbage cans, and people would say, "Oh that's terrible."''

Musicians, on the whole, are not good with reality. They play music that commemorates the glory and horror of war – from the 1812 to Britten's *War Requiem* – and yet to touch it, to be touched by it seems indelicate, an interruption to the serenity of art for art's sake. It is embarrassing, somehow uncivilized, that Wissam's mother is living with exploding bombs and street fighting while through it all running an art gallery. There is little place in musicians' daily small talk for thoughts about patriotism, loyalty or those who have given their lives. Wissam responds by outwardly emphasizing the puckish qualities of his instrument, those that are the most pleasing: the silvery tone, the prettiness of much of what it does, the Pan-like beauty. 'People think I'm extremely extroverted and even I get embarrassed at some of the things I do. But I feel it's my duty to be totally open – what matters to me in music is the raw feeling and the purest of sounds.'

Wissam Boustany

He is a young zealot: 'Idealism is to me totally real. It is a very great responsibility to play a musical phrase. Music is alive, it is important that you are not slaughtering it. So often people say music is a form of self-expression – I believe it is much greater than that. I feel it is an expression of everything around us. Imagine being able to play a phrase that would inspire someone to see a sunset?' Of course they patronize him in the London Symphony Orchestra, talk of him as a gifted sprite who will grow up.

It is more involved: he has come from the Arab world, rooted in violence, mysticism and a simplicity forged from survival in the desert or at sea. The LSO, like so many symphony orchestras, is rooted in the nice, white middle-class experience of front gardens, guest towels and small mortgages. When it thinks of war, it remembers Dame Myra Hess playing lunchtime concerts through the Blitz. At a pinch, it thinks of Jacqueline du Pré and Daniel Barenboim getting married in 1967. Wissam went back to Beirut a while ago, invited to play, of all things, a Gilbert and Sullivan opera. The conductor was shot dead the night before he arrived. No wonder Wissam's stepfather put his violin away for ten years; he felt that music had lost its voice for him.

Wissam talks of playing 'from heart to heart'. The flute is not naturally a physically immediate instrument. The mouth never touches it: there is nothing to suck or to blow, nothing to vibrate or to make a sound of its own. Everything depends on the strength of the muscles poised above the mouth-piece; it is not an old man's instrument. It suggests the piping of a young voice, not the complex and wrinkled character of age. 'The flute', Wissam says, 'has got a nice sound and that's it. But it is the instrument that's closest to nature, that has always been associated with mystic things and with death.'

All around the bedroom of his cold and shabby flat, he has posted exhortations to himself: 'Challenge yourself', 'Practise, you self-satisfied bastard', 'Perfection', 'You must not be afraid of being tired', 'To withhold your energy is to be dead'. Two huge blue plastic bags full of clothes await a trip to the laundry. Somewhere under the mess and disorder, his tails lie in need of cleaning and pressing. A lime-green plastic suitcase is in the middle of the room, always packed and at the ready. In the next few weeks, he will be playing *Lohengrin* with the London Symphony at the Edinburgh Festival, a competition in Paris, a recital in Norfolk and he hopes to go to Beirut.

Wissam misses playing with the ECYO; next year, presumably, he will be too old for it. 'Going on tour with that orchestra is going on an orgy of hysterical happiness.' In the ECYO he plays first, the glory of initiating phrases is all his. In the LSO, he will sit second to Peter Lloyd. 'I think I'm a good second flute' – he is not boasting but anxiously hoping it is so. 'I know how it helps to have a friend supporting you by your side, knowing when to be encouraging and what it means not to shoot someone down at the wrong moment. Peter gives you confidence; he's so nice about what he asks for. When he sits in that chair, he is a real king. He knows what he's going to

Peter Lloyd, *Royal Albert Hall, London*

Peter Francis, *Manchester*

sound like in the hall and he's always ready to sacrifice his own sound to blend better into the orchestra. There is so much to learn from him.'

The LSO first called on Wissam five months ago. He has two friends in the orchestra now: Peter Lloyd and Claudio Abbado. In rehearsal breaks, he seeks the latter out for that is the way it always was in the European Community Youth Orchestra. He will learn. He has already learned much. 'In an orchestra, it is very important to be reliable and to make people around you feel secure. But playing the flute inspires me to face myself and most of the time it is not a pleasant picture.

I don't believe in time, it isn't measurable. I believe only in moments. Playing with Claudio is such a moment. I don't care if I live 300 years or 25 – I want only to make sure my years are alive not half asleep.'

The Friends' Meeting House in Euston Road is opposite the large railway terminus of the same name. Various members of the LSO can time to the second how long it takes to dart across the road, scuttle through the crowds to the station buffet and back again. That is the kind of preparation and experience an orchestra member needs in order to survive and to keep out of trouble. If he looks after the refreshments, goes the reasoning, the conductor can look after the musical fare, in today's case 'bleeding Wagner', as it is quickly and popularly labelled. As a rule, symphony orchestra players are not given to much enthusiasm for opera – indignation, perhaps, at all that toiling underground performed by their brethren in the opera house pit or just a disinclination to work so hard without recognition in the service of singers. In the symphony concert it is the orchestra that is the star. More significantly, musicians, especially string players, dislike music that goes on and on, that is hard and heavy going.

This whole week is devoted to sectional rehearsals for the second act of *Lohengrin* – which it is hoped will be the LSO's Edinburgh Festival show stopper. That is the challenge of international festivals: to find something grandiose or unusual enough to stand out in the crowd of other orchestras and presentations. Work is slacker for the LSO in summer and for once Claudio can have almost all the rehearsal time he wants. Nine hours a day, section by section – an extraordinary luxury.

It is the morning after the ECYO Prom. It has been noted that the reviews of it are good. Those in the LSO who think about such things feel rather older this morning as they get ready to meet Claudio; they are all too aware of the contrast with his young eager beavers. The strings are called first; brass and winds will gather at six this evening. Seventy string players have been booked for *Lohengrin*, 10 more than usual but 22 extras will be sitting in. For some members, August is still holiday time with the family but a few have arranged to be away because they hate Wagner. These latter at least thought ahead. It is unlikely that anyone here has prepared for today. Orchestra members are

Henry Greenwood, *Henry Wood Hall, London*

Triumph at the Edinburgh Festival with Claudio Abbado

always complaining about being bored but it is odd how little responsibility most of them take for their own musical life. What interest can there be in playing the notes of one's own part without any inkling of the overall structure? To play an opera without having studied the score, listened to a recording or, at the very least, read the words through in English has as much satisfaction as fixing one screw on the factory bench.

Everyone knows vaguely about *Lohengrin* – 'knights and honour' as a violinist puts it. Few have any idea what goes on at any particular moment, to what words or action all those heavy string passages will be providing the undercurrent. What, if anything, will the brass be up to at that spot where the strings are twisting their fingers in another of those fiendish high position Wagner phrases? Will there be a great flourish from behind to cover up the detail? Or nothing? A bar is marked pianissimo. What does 'very soft' mean? It is meaningless out of context. There is one level of soft when strings are playing alone, another level when they play beneath a singer, and still another if the brass is blowing in the background. Ah, the pitfalls of just doing one's job with the maximum of competence and the minimum of curiosity!

It starts well enough because everyone is in such a good mood. The sun is shining on the endeavour and, for once, daylight comes into the room in a soft, warm haze without blinding half a section somewhere. (It is a miracle that all musicians do not suffer from headaches and failing eyesight considering the conditions under which they have to peer for hours on end at tiny dots on a distant page.) And, for once the strings are going to be heard. Chamber orchestras often feel this way; it is the attraction of a small, like-minded group that sees itself as playing together, not against one another. Violins, violas, cellos and double basses may squabble among themselves and vie for importance, but they are one family of instruments and feel their kinship. Too often they see their very best efforts are just a backdrop for wind solos or rasping brass. If there is one thing that string players resent it is a conductor's signal to the brass to play still more loudly.

Sectional rehearsals, common enough in student orchestras, are almost unknown to professional ones: too expensive, for a start. They are also slightly offensive to an orchestra, suggesting that there may be room for improvement, scope for a more thorough investigation of the job in hand. Claudio Abbado has no such reworking in mind; he seems content merely to run through the notes again and again. He knows this orchestra too well to have hoped for any private practice to have gone beforehand into the trickier corners of Wagner. He has his own way of working with the LSO; it is subtle, and time and again he slips around a possible confrontation. Just about anyone can stare him down. His criticism is always made by inference: he stops, says nothing or just a word or two before asking for a passage again. He leaves it up to the musicians to see what went wrong. His touch is delicate; he leads not by a show of disapproval but by the withdrawal of his favour. The effect is the same: no one likes to make a mistake around Claudio.

There are many ways to work with your own orchestra. The famous orchestra builders of the past were whip-crackers: George Szell, Fritz Reiner, Artur Rodzinski, Toscanini. They destroyed as many good artists as they trained, if truth be told. To be a disciplinarian is not synonymous with being nasty, not today at any rate. It means only being firm and exacting in the fundamentals of orchestra performance. It means listening carefully for the accuracy of ensemble, encouraging sensitivity to other aspects of the score (what is the second trumpet playing there?), watching out for intonation and taking the trouble to stop when it is shaky, tuning instruments separately if necessary – and all this as matter-of-factly as though it were a question of fine polish, not an act of divine retribution.

Intimidation and shame are strong weapons but in the end self-defeating. The underlying problem that besets all orchestras is the individual's conviction: 'I am only one player – I can't make any difference.' The moment that feeling of insignificance turns to real insecurity, a player becomes tentative. He plays late because he is trying to follow everyone else instead of playing right into a phrase. It takes self-assurance to come in without the security blanket of hearing everyone else first. Self-confidence is the most important ingredient in the making of any successful orchestra. When an orchestra sounds ragged, when its entrances sound uneven and muffled, it is so often assumed that it is because of musical slovenliness, that fifty strings have, of one accord, deliberately chosen to play badly. Every orchestra wants to sound wonderful: believing that it does so is half of it.

Faith healing, however, only goes so far. Orchestra work is painstaking stuff; it means settling down with one hundred per cent concentration to work slowly and thoroughly on details. A good orchestra builder is a conductor who suggests that the responsibility is not his alone but the whole orchestra's. He must have both patience and the ability to transmit this patience to the players. Mystic passion is all very well; hard work and tenacity is what improves an orchestra. The key is never to let the players get bored. Alas, six hours of Wagner will in itself bore the LSO.

There are beautiful phrases here and there and, at first, this is enough. Each time such a phrase comes the mood of the whole rehearsal lightens. String players love to play a passage that has a yearning and vocal beauty to it, and to play it well. But Wagner is rhythmically very complicated; there are long and heavy string passages that are taxing to read and to follow. The music swells and falls, on and on. It starts to feel stuffy in the room. It does not take long for the old LSO reaction to set in: the whispering, the jokes, the high E 'pizz' of a Mighty Mouse somewhere in the first violins that breaks up a difficult and tiresome passage. Mike Davis does not even bother to look round. He knows who is at the centre of all that frenetic good humour. 'Old Mavis,' says Gillian Findlay later with a certain satisfaction, 'I'm a thorn in his flesh.'

When Gillian Findlay joined the LSO five years ago, its only woman member was the Latvian harpist, Renata Scheffel-Stein, a law unto herself. Gilly as a violinist was the first woman to be admitted into the chaps-only ranks. She was 23 years old and, by all accounts, a terrific player. She had just finished four years at Bloomington, Indiana, one of America's top music schools. When she came back to Britain, both the London Philharmonic and the London Symphony offered her a job. 'I thought the LSO would be more of a challenge,' she says, a telling enough explanation.

Snaps of her taken in America show a slender, blonde girl, very pretty and young, all enthusiasm and bright eyes. It must have been exciting to see the little British girl holding her own against the Americans with her big technique and sound. She had been marked out early as a special talent; at 13, her mother used to take her from Glasgow to London by train at weekends so that she could study privately with the right teacher. At 16, she left home and went to the Royal Academy in London. Lonely? It is not a word she acknowledges. 'I always tend to like where I am. Everyone in the States was always going on about having roots. I couldn't give a shit about things like that.' Gillian Findlay, after five years in the London Symphony Orchestra, is a down-to-earth knock-about character.

Her values are her own. Foremost on her blacklist are orchestra worthies and creeps – those who go up to conductors to thank them for a wonderful experience, those who make a big point on tour of going early to bed. 'All that crap, I hate it. If I'm going to get anywhere, it isn't going to be through that. I like to have a good laugh and you seem to have to project the straight-laced, very keen sort of image to get on these days. I am not very keen on pushy people, which is probably why I'll stay where I am.' Mike Davis, 'Mavis' as she has wickedly nicknamed him, is the natural straight man for her comic turns. He worries a lot and, what is more, allows others to see it. By her standards, he has dampened down the first violin section to such an extent that she has been forced to look elsewhere for her friends. 'I used to hang around with a group of fiddles. The fiddles always used to laugh but they went so quiet that I had to move. Now I hang out with the brass; they laugh a lot and they take things as they come.' On tour, at two o'clock in the morning, in a bar or restaurant, there will be a raucous, good-humoured group, in gales of laughter, to whom the night is young. Gillian Findlay will be there holding her own. After five years, she is truly one of the boys.

Certainly life is easier for her than for most of her colleagues: unmarried, no children, no ties. She has bought a one-bedroomed flat overlooking a marina in West London and a silver-green Sirocco (0-60 mph in a flash) to replace the car that was written off in an accident. She drives fast; she loves cars. 'I should have been a boy,' she says more than once. But stuffed higgledy-piggledy into the cocktail cabinet in the lounge are envelopes and folders full of photographs, souvenirs and scraps of paper saved from the

Robert Retallick, *Barbican, London*

Playing cards, Croydon

past. The music stand is out; she is practising hard for a Purcell Room recital. She expects to lose between £700 and £1000 – a legacy from her grandmother – putting it on. 'Well, I can't have given up minding completely, can I?' she says, before adding inevitably the throwaway: 'It'll be all right if I don't play like a complete shit.'

It is hard to be sure how well she plays these days. One of the protective skins offered to those in the backstands is the knowledge that no one need ever hear them play again if that is their pleasure. Gilly did not want to be lost in the backstands. A while ago there was a vacancy up in the front; it must have taken a lot for her to have asked to try out for it. 'Mavis didn't think I was the type to do it,' she shrugs. 'And if I'm not going to be given any responsibility, I'm not going to take any.'

And when the whispering starts, the stifled laughter betrays a mischievous intelligence at work; Mike Davis knows to expect Gilly Findlay to be there somewhere. It is already part of LSO lore that Gilly Findlay is a naughty girl who is late for rehearsals more often than anyone. She will stagger in dropping her black leather coat on the way, face creased and tired, wispy permed hair dunked in the shower – she has her image to think of. One of the least attractive things about the LSO might be said to be the scenario they have written and helped to fulfil for their first young woman member.

Afternote

The *Lohengrin* performance at the Edinburgh Festival was a great success despite, or perhaps because of, the rows at the final rehearsals up in Edinburgh. The situation was so bad at one point that Claudio Abbado walked out. And yet, like much else, even this was inevitable. Six days of rehearsing had guaranteed an explosion of some kind; there was no other outlet for all the tension building up.

A week later, the LSO and Abbado played a Prom together in London as if nothing had happened. Nicholas Kenyon's review in *The Times* the morning after starts: 'After such a superb, exhilarating performance of Berlioz's *Symphonie Fantastique* as the London Symphony Orchestra gave us at last night's Prom, criticism seems beside the point.' Happily, it was Claudio's first concert as music director. The orchestra presented him with a bottle of champagne in the intermission and the Berlioz after. It was one of those rare evenings in which there is not a hint of sourness anywhere, from anyone. It was a pity, everyone agreed, that Douglas Cummings was not playing principal cello that night. He had gone home from the morning rehearsal with a bad headache. No one yet knew, in the middle of this rejoicing, that Duggie had had a brain haemorrhage. For all the talk of the soul of music, every musician is in the end utterly dependent on a body that may betray him at any moment. Perhaps this knowledge has something to do with that tension that underlies orchestra life. Muscle and flesh are, in the end, so treacherous.

Patrick Vermont, Tom Cook, Douglas Powrie and Jack Steadman *travelling to the Edinburgh Festival*

9: *Putting it on Record*

London, the next morning

Kingsway Hall in Holborn is a very run down, its main entrance has long been barred off, handwritten notices locate the 'gents' and mourn the demise of the public telephone. It would be a sad and depressing place in which to realize great music were it not for the ghosts: more than forty years of historic recordings have taken place here. The lobby may have all the romance of a seaside public convenience but the hall inside gives life and breadth to sound. Musicians thrive in these hidden and secret gardens; they foster that camaraderie that makes for good ensemble playing. Without the excuse of an audience, the energy must come from within. Recording is a cool impersonal business, at best.

It is the morning after the LSO's triumphant Prom concert and the orchestra has been booked by Decca for a Brahms concerto: the violinist is a Russian *émigré*, Boris Belkin, and the conductor is Ivan Fischer of Budapest and Amsterdam. Fischer and the LSO have been working together quite a lot: concerts in London, some of a summer tour in America, part of the World Tour in the Far East.

Ivan Fischer, in music management parlance, is 'an up-and-coming young conductor'. On West 57th St in New York, they talk of him as 'hot'. He has been taken up by the LSO and booked by America's most famous of baton talent spotters, Ernest Fleischmann of the Los Angeles Philharmonic. A career snowballs and Fischer is in demand: a *Clemenza di Tito* in Covent Garden, *La Bohème* in Florence; his diary looks suddenly very good for a young artist. No matter that he is already 32 years old, that he has been under top management in London for over eight years: he is young in the music world's eyes for he seems only just to have come to everyone's attention.

Every orchestra wants to have in the wings a young conductor with recording contracts, some prestigious engagements elsewhere to give him standing and enough free time to be available for cancellations, tours, run-outs, major concerts – and, for preference, still at a modest fee. This may explain why when word goes around of someone new and promising, he can virtually hand-pick his engagements for a year or so. Débuts are easy; it is the re-engagement rate that is the test, being asked back season after season. Some candidates fail here because they disappoint, never quite living up to advance publicity; others because they quickly become too demanding: a Beethoven

Ray Adams, *Barbican, London*

Ninth, a Mahler or two and Kiri Te Kanawa's *Four Last Songs* are a mite impractical. Others still make the cardinal young conductor's error: they start to think of the orchestra musicians as mere tools.

The faces before them blur and the orchestra becomes one entity – putty in ambitious hands. Management makes bookings, they reason, smiling coyly at directors and administrators; musicians do as they are told – and never well enough. Thus whipper-snappers do fall from grace.

Ivan Fischer, it would seem, is still in the seduction stage. He knows that orchestra members need to be wooed. Boyish grins, first name stuff, lots of 'please' and 'thank you'. The recording of the first movement runs by smoothly. The LSO is in a tremendously good mood after last night and the boredom of recording, the constant preoccupation with minutiae, has not begun to tell. The test will come with the second movement: known among wind-players as 'the oboe concerto'.

This Brahms slow movement is the most famous of oboe solos, setting out the first statement of the melody before passing it to the violin. There is in this touching tune a hint of long ago, of the instrument's history as a shepherd's horn. It has the simplicity of an old peasant face, but it is also haunted by the personal and tragic overtones of the modern Romantic time. And besides that, there are not many chances to breathe. It is incredibly difficult to play well. The very moments at which the player is likely to be physically on his last gasp are exactly those where the music is at its most emotionally taxing. Oxygenless serenity is the order of the day.

Anthony Camden is looking a trifle tired and pale this afternoon. Unexpectedly, this is, strangely enough, to be his first Brahms violin concerto on record, so it is as much a test of his musicianship as the solo violinist's. It is the worst kind of test: all over the world oboe players will see the London Symphony Orchestra on the record and put the needle down on the opening of the slow movement. There under the merciless scrutiny of oversized speakers and superpower amplifiers, Anthony Camden's playing will be laid bare and judged. It is not a very nice thought.

In his ubiquitous maroon leather case is a letter from his mother, herself a cellist before she married the greatest bassoon player in England. It is a touching appeal to Anthony to use the next few years to lay down a historical document of his playing, to step aside from the distractions of being Mr Chairman and his involvement with running things. 'I would love one day to be able to be a complete lunatic,' he says, 'but there has to be something in reserve always for the person who is chairman in case things really go wrong.' Ray Still, celebrated first oboe of the Chicago Symphony Orchestra, has recorded the Brahms concerto twice: once with Jascha Heifetz, and again some years ago with Itzhak Perlman. His is a hard act to follow. Boris Belkin has had weeks to prepare for these sessions; Anthony Camden has been playing orchestral concerts and, in between, wooing sponsors to help in this

Ivan Fischer

latest financial crisis. Unwritten etiquette decrees that Anthony should be given whatever support he needs.

Ivan Fischer comes out to start the second session. He asks the wind section to play through the opening statement. They do so: Anthony is marking his solo, saving his stamina for the moment that the red recording light goes on. ('They never use the first take anyway,' he says; clearly he is a man who has been through this often enough to know that in recording endurance is everything.) When the winds finish, there is one of those split seconds in which a conductor has to take a difficult and delicate decision – and gets it wrong.

The maestro asks for it again, obviously planning to stop and start, to rehearse and work on phrasing and detail. Recording needs even more faith than a concert: if there is the safety net of being given more than one chance, there is also the knowledge that a record is for ever (or at least until it is deleted from the catalogue). The energy has to go into the 'takes'. There were alternatives open to Fischer: he could, for instance, have said that it was beautiful, given the oboe a list of points and gone immediately for a take. An old hand like Camden could have absorbed whatever the conductor wanted and reacted accordingly. But Ivan Fischer is newer at the game; he does not know the parameters of the orchestra and cannot trust a player enough for that. He still believes that it is up to a conductor to make the music.

There were still other ways out: Fischer could have run through his list even believing that it would not work but gone for a take anyway. In the privacy of the playback room next door, he and Camden could have listened together to the result. Better etiquette by far to criticize the oboe's playing in private, not in front of his colleagues. It also gets better results, for listening together to a piece of tape makes the whole process less personal; anyway it is much easier for Anthony to hear what needs to be fixed if he is not playing at the same time. An older conductor would never have cornered himself like this at such a tricky moment. But then, a really experienced orchestra man would have had the foresight to telephone Camden for a relaxed chat about the solo, long before the heat was on. It takes confidence to do that – in music, confidence often means only the ability to think of the other man.

Ivan Fischer is probably misled by Mr Chairman's glacial charm at the moment. He may not have the slightest inkling of how on edge the oboe is. There is one of those tensions in the studio now that leads to absolute silence. The only sounds are of the conductor trying to rehearse and rework the solo and, finally, the solo oboist saying, calmly and sensibly, that he may not have the stamina to keep playing over and over again. The winds suddenly have some noisy business among themselves. 'Tony, Tony . . .' says the conductor meaningfully, trying to keep everything on a friendly basis. It is not the best moment to be unaware that he likes to be called Anthony: 'When people rang up at home and asked for "Tony" my mother would always put the phone down on them. She would say: "There's no one here of that name."'

A take, at last. Camden and Fischer go back to hear it with Michael Haas, the Decca producer. They soon return to try again: the pick-up is not strong enough, Anthony remarks. He thinks that on this second try, he is simply playing louder. There is much more involved than that, as there always is. Without consciously trying to, he is responding to everything he heard and that he missed hearing in the playback. His tone is softer and more velvety, the louder moments are fuller, phrasing is freer and more giving, articulations are clearer but also more subtle. He has brought life to the solo.

Fischer does not seem to have grasped the mood of the wind section even now. The conductor wants to rehearse the second part of the wind solo. Now it is Terry Johns, 'Drac', the easy-going horn, playing principal first today, who is starting to fret. Pencils and mutes clatter; much squeaking into reeds and spitting into mouthpieces is going on. Fischer does not look up, he does not raise his voice, but a loaded patience creeps into his tone signalling displeasure. Few conductors, when it comes to it, really understand what it is to play the instruments that they command. How can Ivan Fischer possibly see why Martin Gatt, the bassoon, is so irritable? The bassoon is not doing anything crucial in this spot. Well, not in a concert, perhaps, but any slight deviation of pitch or attack from the bassoon right now would spoil the overall effect of the recording. It is nerve-racking for a player to have to try a phrase over and over again like this, hoping that when it comes to a take that works for the principal concerned – the horn or oboe – he will not have to say, 'Oh, I think I played a wrong note there.' In a concert, such mistakes happen all the time. Recording is about achieving a spontaneity and cold perfection in the same split second.

A horn player's lip is fragile. 'Drac' is nervous now because he has had to blow too often and too long to feel secure. By the time the red light goes on again for a take, the atmosphere in the studio is less than electrifying. As the players seem to hang back, staring blankly at him, the conductor tries to emote more, waving his long arms with increasingly large gestures, reacting to every swelling phrase with fervent facial expressions. Orchestra players call this 'stirring the soup'. It has the unfortunate result of slowing everything up. Reacting is in the past tense, it is behind the momentum of the music which then starts to drag. Another listening session; Fischer returns briskly. 'It's a bit slow,' he announces. It surprises no one. 'How about conducting quicker?' comes a suggestion from the back.

It is just the usual conductor-orchestra relationship – when is it not fraught with misunderstandings?

10: The Longest Day

Henry Wood Hall, London, Saturday morning

Films, jingles, pop backing tracks: they lead inexorably to Classic Rock. The title is identified with the London Symphony Orchestra but is not its property. It is in the hands of the marketing team that invented the idea and, to all intents and purposes, controlled artistically by them. Four Classic Rock albums have been released and sold between them 3.5 million copies; it is worth £60,000 a year in royalties to the Orchestra Ltd. Most of its musicians think it is fun to play and most of them appreciate the money. A few have pointedly arranged to be released from the Classic Rock concert coming up this week.

'The Eye of the Tiger' belted out on stage in an ice hockey stadium in Sweden is not everyone's notion of acceptable music-making for a symphony orchestra. It is interesting that Claudio Abbado has two rehearsals later today for a Brahms Requiem coming up at the Festival Hall. No one has found it necessary to mention to him that the LSO will be pounding away at Classic Rock for three hours beforehand. It is one thing to run with the heavy leather set, another to boast of it.

The orchestra is currently going through a version of 'Baker Street'. Rock musician, Raf Ravenscroft, 29, alumnus of Stoke-on-Trent and the Royal College of Music, is famed among those who know such things for his solo work on the hit record. He is here today, wandering up and down the stands of the LSO, saxophone in hand, stopping now and again as the spirit moves him to deliver himself of a plaintive wail or two. He is a splendid sight: black leather trousers, high-heeled black leather boots, plum silk shirt, gold ornaments and silky auburn curls. He has a large, hairy, roguish face; he looks like some pirate king supervising the lowly subjects busying themselves with their tasks. Next to him, all those nice LSO members look like miniatures of Englishmen, pinched, drawn and occupied with matters of the mind. It is odd how little outward awareness classical musicians present of their physical selves beyond the rigours of those disciplined muscles with which they play.

They walk and move as they play: at their most free, they shamble. None of them has – or perhaps dares to have – the swagger and strut, the loose-limbed padding about of the visitors here this morning from the rock 'n roll world. These visitors betray themselves at one glance: they are mostly thin, youthfully dressed but with one or two crucial items that signal money. Upon their spotless scalps they bear the mark of the trichology clinic and custom-made shampoos.

The orchestra is a curious mix at this point too. Dotted within it are the session musicians, rock men, sitting in on the rhythm section or keyboard. They bob and sway, moving into the music as it drives forward. There is a brief sense of *déjà vu*. The European Community Youth Orchestra – that is it. The ECYO looked something like this, all those young gleaming, tossing heads and gesturing arms, all the very kind of emotive swaying about that older, professional musicians find exasperating and a distraction.

Is it just another part of the generation gap? Those who remember Jascha Heifetz playing like an eagle on the watch will complain, probably, that Kyung Wha Chung's much freer stance 'gets in the way of the music': the one-size-fits-all complaint used to express any form of disapproval about almost anything. There are others, younger for the most part, who equate stillness with coldness and who value above all other qualities excitement for its own sake. The epitome of 'excitement' nowadays is not the latest in violin prodigies but a rock musician such as Raf Ravenscroft whose playing springs totally from the momentum of the music, from the guts of it not from some pre-ordained structure. (How, a rock musician may ask, can a violinist playing his hundredth Tchaikovsky concerto still feel genuine excitement at exactly the same place when he has played that spot time and time again?)

When a concept is bigger than any individual's contribution, as in Classic Rock, it is not going to matter too much who is conducting as long as there is a certain level of competence. On the records, each arranger has conducted his own piece. Someone has to keep the thing together. The conductor for the Swedish concert is a tactful bow to the LSO and something of a compromise: a young, long-haired composer-arranger called Richard Harvey. It is an inspired thought: Richard writes jingles and understands the commercial world, but he also plays the baroque recorder and conducts evenings of 'authentic' early music. He is a serious sort with long sensitive hands and poky arms that he waves towards the orchestra rather as a kindly vicar would conduct the ladies' choir. He is still an LSO type of chap.

After the break a guest star comes to the podium. Jeff Wayne is an American who first came to London in 1953 when his father, Jerry Wayne, starred in the West End (Sky Masterson, *Guys and Dolls*). He is show business; he grew up with it. He is the composer, originator, producer and conductor of the double album 'War of the Worlds'. ('I don't like to quote figures, but let's say it cost £125,00 to make and that it has grossed $40 million so far and that it has been number one in ten countries.') The electricity is instant: no knee-bend here to the classical style; this is hard and driving rock, raw and gutsy: everything that is an anathema to the realization of classical music. It is also irresistible.

'Rock 'n roll', says the white-faced onlooker from behind his dark sunglasses, 'is pure aggression.' The idea clearly delights him. John Kurlander was the recording engineer on the Classic Rock records. He will mastermind 111 individual microphones wired to a console under his control when Classic Rock gets to Gothenburg. In his time, John Kurlander has captured the august sound of the Philadelphia Orchestra for EMI records. As he relishes the beat of 'War of the Worlds', he says happily: 'This is where I really come from – this is my background.' The musicians sitting out there, working away, are merely his raw material. After a lifetime spent staring at musical notation, deciphering its exact mathematics, and measuring their days in dots and bars, the orchestra musicians are finally letting rip at the simplest, most basic level. They are generating the energy to be formed and moulded by John Kurlander.

It is to be expected that for some there is only relief at finally relinquishing responsibility. They may scrape and saw, knowing that subtlety and restraint can for once be totally forgotten. Classical music is a precious world; at times it seems no more than an affectation, a pose supported by the rich and pretentious. 'With all due respects,' says Tony Prior, the father of and brains behind Classic Rock, 'I think the classical side of music is mad; it is so uncommercial.' Obviously, Tony Prior believes that what is happening here today makes sense. The LSO, as he talks, is playing through another number from the programme for Gothenburg: it is 'Reach out', an old Four Tops hit that came from Tamla Motown records. One hundred or so musicians are commemorating a piece of music that has every ounce of its fibre rooted in the black experience. In the hall there is not one black face. Never has the remoteness of classical music from the world outside seemed so tangible.

Saturday lunchtime
It is lunchtime in the crypt; in the canteen kitchen a pot of something nondescript is warming on the range. Upstairs, as if by magic, the forest of cymbals, drum kits, synthesizers and electric guitars have been spirited off into cases and vans. Henry Greenwood the librarian, who is not on duty for Classic Rock, is taking possession of the music stands once again, smoothing on to them the parts for this afternoon. The wild hours are over; it is time once again for the serious and the painstaking stuff. The prospect seems dull by comparison. The morning's driving beat and simple, searching tunes were very alluring. It is tedious to have to scale everything down again, to have to go back to that fussy precision.

The crypt is almost empty. It is a lovely, sunny day and all that vibrant jumping and shaking has sent many musicians outside to explore the world – or perhaps they are trying to recover out in the open from noise exhaustion. Meanwhile downstairs, at the quiet tables, there is hardly a violinist or wind player in sight. But over there against the wall, predictably enough, is the little bunch of viola players who somehow always find one another.

No one ever talks much about the viola section. It is with orchestras as it is with families: being worthy and being good usually have to be their own reward. Being reliable is an invitation to being taken for granted. The viola section is the most stable in the LSO: the front desk has not changed for over ten years. Alec Taylor, the principal, has a reputation for leading like the gentleman Scot he is. Alec Taylor, say his admiring band of extras, is the one leader for whom no one need fear playing out. He has himself a deep, full tone and newcomers to his section are asked to have their instruments set up to favour the lower registers. He wants a big sound from the men behind him. Cannily, he gets it by never asking. Of all the LSO principals, he seems to say the least in rehearsal about anything. He sits there and plays – rock solid. 'If I think it needs more,' he says, 'mebbe I'll turn round and give a look. I never say it's too loud, I leave that to the Boss. In that way, I like to be positive.'

For the most part the violas are the inner voice of the string section. They lie between the brilliance of the violins and the mellowness of the cellos; it takes a special character to know how to blend with both. A good viola section is one that can play the bass deeply when the cello has the melody and can play so brightly with the second violins when needs be that it is impossible to tell the difference. To do all that well, to do it 'behind the scenes' needs a personality that can give and take, easily and generously. The distinctive viola sound of the LSO stands out for musicians – too often in an orchestra, that middle voice is no more than a nasal, scratchy sound.

To the bass instruments the violins are Mad Hatters and hares, the lot of them. Viola players are the thoughtful ones. It is easy to see in an orchestra when there are viola players who have come to the instrument as failed violinists, making the most of a second choice. They have thin, spindly fingers, and the larger viola juts out of their neck like an awkward-sized box. Often, the true viola player has bigger hands, fingers slightly larger than would be comfortable for the fiddle. The viola is his natural instrument and he wraps himself around it somewhat in the way that cellists do. Alec Taylor is that kind of viola player and those are the players he likes behind him.

Every now and again, there is a solo, a phrase, sometimes just a particular attack, that suddenly exposes the violas. It always comes as a surprise to catch the deep strong sound of the LSO section; it is probably the strongest and most disciplined part of the LSO. An orchestra can have flabby violas and still be wonderful but it comes as a kind of bonus, say in Mahler, suddenly to hear from the middle such fullness and such playing.

Often it is easier to see what a particular player is striving for when you know who are his musical heroes. Alec Taylor cites two: William Primrose who was so strong that he once lifted up his accompanist using not his arms but his hands alone. Lionel Tertis is the other, just over 5 feet tall but with such phenomenal strength that he played a viola 17½ inches long. The differences of viola length sound so minuscule to the outsider: Alec Taylor's relief weapon chosen for this long day is a modern, orange viola 16 inches long. He calls it 'little' – they all look the same to those who do not have to hold them up in the air, hour after hour.

Alec's great Italian viola made in 1628 by Antonio Brenzi of Bologna is 17 inches long and weighs 1 lb 10 oz, 3 crucial ounces more than this 'little' one. For very special occasions he brings out a Flemish viola made in 1690 which is 18¼ inches long and a gargantuan 1 lb 13 oz. Of such seemingly unimportant distinctions are bouts of bursitis made, the string player's curse and nightmare. And, of course, Alec Taylor has had his share of trips to the osteopath. What he dreads are the long days when there is a Brahms First Symphony or certain of the Schumann symphonies to rehearse. The great Schubert C Major is not even to be spoken of because it is so tiring for the violas, page after page, bar after bar without a rest.

A section betrays its character in many small but telling ways. When the LSO first violins get tired, for instance, they grow careless. One sure sign of their fatigue is inattentive entries that are not always together or on time. When Alec Taylor's violas start to tire, it shows in the increasing speed with which they drop their violas onto their knee the instant a note is over and even the briefest of rests is upon them. It is on the leaving of the note and not the arriving that they conserve themselves. There is a stoic pride in their service.

The lunch break is nearly over; the next sessions will soon unfold. Alex Taylor finishes his banana and apple, carefully folds the debris and brushes the crumbs into a brown paper bag. He wipes off his hands testing out his fingertips and checks that he is prepared for the next three hours. He is the most patient, resolute and tidy of men – and so he plays.

Saturday afternoon

How quickly the time passes: another break already, another hour to pass before the next session. There is no longer a sense of time flowing, only of lasting it out. A numbness takes over, patches vanish as if they never happened. In the Trinity Arms pub, some players sit, beer glass in hand, staring through this numbness. A snooker game is just winding up among the younger bloods. Three horns stand one another final glasses of red wine. Outside, the German baritone, Hermann Prey, walks round and round Trinity Church Square scuffing the early autumn leaves. The ring of last-minute smokers is already by the door of the Henry Wood Hall, drawing deeply on the penultimate cigarette before Brahms.

The strange light that heralds the dusk is slanting through the tall church windows. The hall is filling up with musicians and chorus members. Anthony Camden is warming up, trying hard not to play any melodic phrase that might attract unnecessary attention. Wissam Boustany, still a guest second flute, on the other hand, is piping for joy. The first player's solos from

Douglas Davenport and David Neale, *Edinburgh*

Arrival of the instruments, Town Hall, Birmingham

something by Tchaikovsky pour out of his silver instrument, carrying mellifluously through the hall. Peter Lloyd, older and wiser, files in and leans over towards Wissam for some important consultation, gently distracting his young partner from this exuberant display. No purple patches today, he decrees: the Brahms Requiem is six movements long. 'It is a piece that must start at the beginning,' says Peter. 'Not too loud and, please, not too beautiful too soon. Everything must build.'

The presence of the chorus gives a charge to the LSO. Musicians always respond to the orchestra of voices behind them, it is natural. They are moved, too, by the knowledge that the chorus members sing not for payment but for the sheer love of doing it – they study, practise and give hours to rehearsing, gladly and eagerly. The LSO chorus lines up now, an astonishing medley of faces, styles, ages and outfits, many of them craning forward with excitement and, perhaps, a tinge of smugness. They are enthusiasts who know that what they are about to do is of considerable importance and that, fully prepared as they are, they will do it well.

Claudio Abbado gives the downbeat and the slow throbbing first movement begins this moving evocation of death, sorrow and consolation. A spectrum of emotions have been played out in this hall today: Classic Rock to the Brahms German Requiem; the celebration of the flesh, the submitting to eternity.

> Lord, make me to know mine end
> and the measure of my days,
> what it is; that I may know
> how frail I am.

It is dark outside as Hermann Prey stands to sing these words; it is magnificent and also humbling.

Footnote: Review by Hilary Finch in *The Times*

'Brahms's Requiem found the orchestra acutely responsive, and the London Symphony Chorus a worthy match for some of their worthiest playing. Mr Abbado found a rare flexibility and strength within the work's life-pulse, sharpening its focus with bright inner detail.'

There were empty seats at all prices; sometimes, it is hard not to be discouraged.

A minor Classic Rock
En route to Sweden, Tuesday afternoon

Mike Frye, the LSO's long-time principal percussion and a member of its board of directors, always looks the odd man out on tour. He is slight with long bushy hair, a beard and a dazzling line in white sports clothes. He is not everybody's idea of a serious musician, not to look at anyway. That he was pop star Mike Oldfield's drummer for four years seems to fit his image much better. For once it is Mike who seems perfectly turned out for the occasion and the other members who look out of place. Mike Frye is playing drums for Classic Rock and he has with him his wardrobe of jeans, leather tennis sneakers and T-shirts. Surprisingly, this will be his début in the role for Classic Rock. 'I didn't think they could afford me quite honestly.'

His days of moonlighting between rock and the LSO are over. When he played regularly in a rock band he ran three or four miles a day and did karate in order to keep in shape for its demands. 'It's a lot of effort and I'm not a kid any more. When I was 27 or 28, I could do a three- hour rock show but now I'm 33 and I reckon I feel it. Psychologically, when I sit down behind a drum kit, I expect to be paid what I got when I was with Oldfield – I won't do it for the regular concert fee.'

Mike Frye professes a certain independence of thought as befits the joint proprietor of F & H Percussion Ltd of Wapping, the Malandela Management Company and the pop recording label, Solid Records. 'I could sell up my house and my companies tomorrow and retire. I would think nothing of it. It would only take a few things to go wrong and I'd feel too old to fight. I've got a car worth more than most people's houses. I've got a house worth more than most people's lifelong income and I've got a flat in Florida. I would never like to feel chained or caged up anywhere.'

He is a bright man. As he settles into his seat on the 1.45 train from Victoria Station to Gatwick Airport, it does not escape his notice that LSO players stream past the window and that none of them stops to get in. 'Look around me, I'm not exactly surrounded by my friends, am I?' Orchestra musicians might not find it easy to accept a colleague whose Rolls-Royce cost more than their semi-detacheds in the suburbs. It is hard not to be resentful, or jealous or simply embarrassed by it all. It must be hard, too, to see that confident, cocksure Mike is not unlike the small boy at boarding school with the too big tuck box longing to be liked. His mother was a violinist, his father was a viola player with the Royal Liverpool Philharmonic for thirty years. That was the world he grew up with and that background goes deeper than rock 'n roll, deeper than the power of employing pluggers and PRs. It explains why, after all these years, he still turns up for the LSO, why he is so earnest about it and why he is aware that he is not in the orchestra's inner ring.

This ring never has anything to do with responsibility or artistic importance: it never does in any orchestra. Why is anyone ever popular? But somewhere on this train are small groups of players, laughing, swapping jokes, sharing lives or just being tired together, and Mike Frye is not among them. This is not to say that his colleagues do not wish him well. He is still one of them. They are delighted that 'their' chap will be the big star of Classic Rock this week – in so far as anyone will see him behind the thick wall of cymbals and drums lined up in front of his stool in centre stage.

It will not be quite like old times for him: 'This is all very tame pseudo rock, really.' It is not like the helicopter rides of yore with Oldfield down into the screaming crowds: 60,000 in Knebworth two years ago, 350,000 once in Madrid. ('It is the most exciting thing that could ever happen to an individual and it's gone in 2½ hours.') A rock band's drummer is its metronome, its pace-setter; he is not the also-ran to a lead guitar. If he goes wrong the whole group goes to pieces. In rock, rhythm is everything. In an orchestra, only a conductor is meant to take that role and importance upon himself.

'Believe me, it was very hard to relate to doing gigs with Oldfield and taking all that cash and then going back to playing the triangle in the Brahms Haydn Variations and having a conductor tell you you're too loud, too soft or, worst of all, not in tempo.' Mike Frye, who once flew everywhere with Mike Oldfield by private jet, five star all the way, who has known what it is to make the musical decisions, is travelling second class to Gatwick Airport to catch DA 8000, the Dan Air charter to Gothenburg. A snack will be available on board.

The lounge around the departure gate at Gatwick airport is so quiet that later LSO arrivals look around anxiously, worried that the plane must have left. Crosswords are being tackled, newspapers, a whispered chat or two about what was said to the bank manager. ('I persuaded him it's all temporary – well, it is all temporary, isn't it?') It is an unexpectedly peaceful scene; trips abroad do not usually start like this.

A Classic Rock concert in Gothenburg is nothing to get worked up about; it is no test of artistry, no critical judgements are involved and besides, in Sue Mallet's words, 'It's a bit of a doddle, isn't it?' There will be nothing to do from six o'clock this evening when the buses get to the hotels and three tomorrow afternoon. For this unaccustomed day of rest plus one three-hour rehearsal and a concert, the lordly sum of two concert fees will be paid plus 350 Swedish kronor subsistence for 1.5 days, bed and breakfast. This is a treat, a well-deserved treat, and most members of the LSO feel that they owe it to themselves to enjoy it.

For most, it is a question of being relaxed for once. For a few, it is a sad time. Douglas Cummings, the principal cellist is recovering from an eight-hour brain operation. Among those close to Duggie, those who went at once to see him in hospital, there is an aftermath of shock and concern. Duggie has a 2-year-old son. His wife is expecting their second baby in four months. Some of the LSO went in to see Duggie before the operation when the outlook was still uncertain. His courage touched them all. 'Duggie, of all people' is what everyone says again and again.

Will Lang, the veteran owl-faced trumpet player, has a wistful and anxious look about him too. His particular friend on tours has always been Donald Stewart, the second violinist. But Donald had a slight heart attack a day or so ago and is at home in bed. Poor Will Lang, he looks so lost. Donald is 58, a bad age to have this tap on the shoulder. And even Anthony Camden looks less than his usual, ineffably confident self. In his case, there is another more unexpected reason as well.

He is Archie Camden's son. One cannot imagine what that great bassoon player would have made of the pounding into a hundred mikes of Classic Rock. 'My father had a code of discipline and perfection,' Anthony has said, 'and as long as you didn't fall below it, there was no problem.' Some of the orchestra are looking forward to tomorrow's concert, but not he. He denies it but Anthony Camden has his Achilles' heel; there is, deep down, something of the artistic snob in him. For the same reason that he has fought to keep that aristocratic purist, Claudio Abbado, with the LSO, he is a bit ashamed of what he is doing. As Mr Chairman, he knows how grateful the LSO should be for the income and for the exposure; as a musician, he squirms as any other artist might. And the more he smiles bravely through it during the next two days, the more endearing it is to see him flinch. He is at his most vulnerable on this trip to Gothenburg; that thick skin he worked hard to acquire to cover his public schoolboy shyness cannot help him here.

Like many British players, including Peter Lloyd the principal flute, he originally took up a wind instrument as 'medicine' for his asthma. In Anthony's case, he had had double pneumonia at 5 and was so sickly that he did not start school until he was 8. He must have struggled and disciplined himself unbelievably to have achieved his technique. At times, he clearly misses some of the imagination and freedom of spirit that he has deliberately put in a straitjacket because of other responsibilities. He said once, in a glorious muddle of images, 'I think it's much more important in a symphony orchestra to have your technical area sorted out than all the stuff about the old hair on the back standing up because in an orchestra like this, you can't afford to take risks. Taking the top off the old lemonade bottle is marvellous, it's terrific, but what an orchestra needs is a principal who is so steady that he's like a shuttle that docks immediately. Anyway, that is exactly what is required for me.'

In the briefcase he is carrying with him there is a tape tucked away by request. It is the Strauss Oboe Concerto he played with the LSO and Fischer after a whole week of nothing else but practising for his own solo concert. 'I think if I may say so, it's a bit freer and not at all bad. "Reliable" – well, it's not much of a compliment, is it?'

The dull importance of being reliable is even more on Anthony Camden's mind than usual these days. His work this summer with the European Community Youth Orchestra underlined the constant predicament facing every orchestra: *when* is old enough? And its corollary: when is too old? 'Everyone in the orchestra,' he says, 'whether they like me or thoroughly dislike me, they all know there's one person whose job it is to be the executioner: me.' There is even now a small list of players to be encouraged diplomatically to move aside over the next few years, just as there is always someone to whom the chance to move up should or should not be offered. When is 'ready'? When is 'ready enough'? To make the wrong decision at the wrong moment is always to risk either losing or breaking a good player.

The principal first horn's seat, as it happens, is still empty. For once, there is an obvious contender within the orchestra but this opening has come a vital year or so too soon for him – at least as the chairman sees it.

Richard Bissell is 23 years old and another of Jim Brown's graduates. He first went to study with him privately when he was 13 and stayed until he graduated from the Royal Academy of Music two years ago. Richard has learned not only how to play the horn beautifully, but he has absorbed music from a large and generous orchestra man. Jim Brown knows it all: the solos, the parts, the tricky spots, the dodges, the strains. And, on top of that, he also understands how an orchestra fits together, personally as well as musically. As chairman of the Royal Philharmonic Orchestra years ago, he watched over that orchestra through times that were at least as difficult as these. There are good reasons why he is Professor James Brown, OBE.

Natural talent by definition cannot be taught and Richard Bissell's is an extraordinary one. It is a unique gift to be able to move, as he can, between the high first and third horns and the low second and fourth. Almost every player in the world has to choose between them. The LSO is trying hard not to exploit him; it wants to protect him and give him time. John Fletcher's admonition about 'dustbowl farming' needs no repeating in this case. Richard Bissell, brought along carefully enough, could take care of the LSO's horn future for years. Too much responsibility too soon, reasons Anthony, might spoil it. In its time, the LSO has taken a chance on young talents such as he, fresh from college. Duggie Cummings was only 20 when he was appointed as principal cello but the first cellist's solos are few. There is always time to learn them ahead. There are symphonies and concertos in which every page has some special moment for the horn. A recording studio is no place for a principal horn to learn his stuff. There is no substitute for knowing the notes, for having sorted out enough of the repertoire to be able to rely on experience not on inspiration.

All well and good. The talk is of finding some distinguished veteran who might come in and nurse young Richard through the next few years: Myron Bloom, George Szell's legendary horn from the Cleveland Orchestra, is one name that is being mentioned. There is a European tradition and a knowledge of the entire literature that such a player could pass on. Working on orchestral excerpts in college, even playing first horn in the Leicestershire Schools Symphony Orchestra, as Richard did, is not the same as sitting in the LSO week after week, country after country.

The flaw in all this logic is Richard Bissell. He does not believe that he needs a musical nanny; he does not wish to be protected. At 23, small, with a tufty moustache that he has been growing for six years, Richard sees himself as an adult, married man, and rather more reliable than some of the insecure and ageing stars in the music profession. 'I'm not saying I want to be *the* principal horn but would at least like to share it for a while,' he says earnestly. 'It all boils down to how you play – if you start splitting notes, people start piling on the pressure. But I'm very calm, I don't panic about things, I regard myself as a stable sort of bloke and honestly, I think I could do it.'

There is an amazing and cool confidence that only a first-rate player has and, often enough, only while he is still young enough to see the future as an ally. Richard Bissell has, by his own admission, never bothered to listen to or study Denis Brain's recordings. 'It has not really interested me who the big players are. I've sort of got on and done it myself. I mean, I don't think there's anything wrong with *my* sound – it's all individual, isn't it?' Jim Brown is about the only older player to command his wholehearted respect. 'There are not many men that age still playing, are there?'

As far as he is concerned, *he* will be different. He will not fall to pieces, run into a bad patch or stray from home and the bigger view of life. 'If you've got someone to go home to, that sort of thing, it keeps you sane. I like playing the nice, juicy tunes but I also like arranging, composing, playing the piano. There's more to music than playing the horn, you know. These people have got nothing else to do except play their instrument until they retire. I look at "them" and say I'm just not going to be like them. If you can get out while you're still on top, that's the thing to do. Life's too short to worry about petty little things like whether your lip is going to crack. I see people who get spots and cold sores and cracks. I've never had them. I think if you go around worrying about your mouth, you're in trouble.'

It is the young man's cry: it will never happen to me.

Gothenburg, Wednesday morning

Over the weeks, the individual faces of the LSO have begun to stand out. Some, even now, come to mind immediately; some never do. It is like any self-enclosed world; to enter it is to recognize the rich skeins that tie it together. How can an orchestra not have its own unique personality? It is composed of so many different characters, some more talented, some less, some errant, some timid, but almost all of them questioning and complex. There are, again as in all such worlds, certain taboos, subjects that are never brought up. There are always one or two players who are never talked of for there is a tacit conspiracy to shelter them. They are protected by the strong and go unnoticed by the weak.

Anthony Chidell, second horn, is one of these. He is 41, slender, greying, quiet around those who do not know him and handsome in a dark, damaged kind of way. He is a great second horn. In Mozart, where the music is always written for a pair of horns, he is able to blend with the top and float his own bottom line with incredible softness and delicacy. He joined the London Philharmonic when he was 20, after a year with the London Mozart Players: he was a talent to watch. He came to the LSO in 1971. Outsiders sometimes ask why such a terrific horn player has never played first. Those who heard him long ago say he certainly could have done so; he chose not to.

Every now and again, Tony Chidell suggests that he would like to talk of the orchestra. Others have said the same and, too often, it has turned out to be more orchestra gossip. On the morning of the Classic Rock concert, Tony Chidell turns up tentatively and apologizes for having nothing to offer after all. He stays for a mug of coffee and talks. This is what he has to say:

'I was asked by Barry Tuckwell to be his second horn in 1966 with this orchestra but unfortunately my brother had just committed suicide. He went flying out of a window. I often go to look at the paving stone where he died. So that's why I didn't join the LSO sooner. First horn? Oh yes, I could do it all right, I still can. But I've always been aware that my sanity is a fragile thing. I always felt I should play safe and go well inside my ability and stay sane. I love this orchestra and I intend to stay in it.

'I have played here with nine first horns and I've outlasted every single one. The first horn is a ridiculous job but look at the casualty list in an orchestra: first horns, leaders, first trumpets, first oboe, all of them. Anyone who sticks his neck out. Extraordinary courage seems to be the order of the day. It seems so silly doesn't it, to waste so much energy and courage just on sitting in a symphony orchestra?

'These people give the public and the conductor more than they deserve. Especially a conductor, looking down from his several thousand pound fee at someone earning his forty pounds and saying "Do it for me". What I've always loved are these genius musicians, as mad as a hatter, who have lost every job they're ever had. There's always a need to cut down these colourful characters. Now Richard Bissell, he'll be good but will he be great? To be great is to be mad, to be vulnerable, to be completely nuts. Old Anthony Camden is like that – he is actually extraordinarily and airily mad. I like people who are unreal: it is an unreal profession.

'In an orchestra, we're not artists, we're not musicians, we're craftsmen. We're like the stonemason carving an eagle 500 feet up on the roof of a building with more love and more care than anyone would ever know. And that eagle will get rained on and blown on until its beak falls off. You can't go poncing about being an 'artiste', especially as a horn player. It's a very short lifespan as a horn player – you've seen what reed players do to their old reeds? They break them. You see them all over the floor – thrown away, trodden in. This, this flesh is the reed; with the horn, the lip is what vibrates. The top lip has most to do and look at it – there's not much of it, is there? You've got these hard ivories on the one side and this metal on the other and the two are trying to grind down this soft flesh – it's a bastard, the horn. It is a bastard.

'Somehow we are cursed to play with the beautiful and simple line of a boy soprano without any vibrato, a steely cold sound. But if your heart is racing through fear, it is audible in the sound. This is very humiliating to those of us who do not wish to have a heart, or at least in public. If the heart is going too fast, it thumps the lungs so you get the sound of the heart beat in the controlled, steady air column which is what the note is. A person sounds like he is: Murphy is a warm-hearted giver, a goer. That's not the trumpet, that's Murphy.

'When I was 20 I was getting a lot of work and a lot of success and I thought I was only getting the work because I was a beautiful boy whose sensitivity made even me cry. So I stopped trying. No one will ever say, "Good old Tony, he was good once", not about me. No one will ever do me a favour for the sake of the old days. I adore exploring the borderline. But I intend to last out, I intend to play in this orchestra for another 20 years. So the self-destruction rules are extremely fine and structured and delicate, and I adhere to them strictly. I do play as well as I can. Always. And I do behave as badly as I can – always. And if I get the sack, it'll be because I've underestimated the balance between insanity, ability and unacceptable behaviour.

'I'm sure some people would prefer to see someone sitting there who talks of the garden and the wife. Work is so short that we all have to behave well these days. Some people want us to be like the NPO, the Philharmonia – the 'New Pensioners Orchestra'. They're so nice there that someone like me feels nauseous when he goes there. You have a two-note solo to play and they say, "Oh, good luck". Give me the LSO any time – they can be marvellously dreadful and they can be great. I'll tell you, the biggest insult you can give the LSO is to say this orchestra isn't trying in a concert. It may not always come out right but those characters play their hearts out. In a rehearsal, yes, bad behaviour, blowing raspberries, drunk if you like – but that's our business, that's private. I really love this orchestra so I've written all my rules so I can stay: keep my mouth shut, play all the notes, take the money and run.'

In every orchestra there are some people whom you should never hurt. They hurt themselves enough and too often. Music is a high risk business; the wrecks are many.

11: Last Farewells

Gothenburg, Wednesday afternoon

The Scandinavium is a vast concrete convention centre set down somewhere in Gothenburg. It is away from the historic port and away from the charm of the old town centre. Last night, there was an ice hockey match here; tomorrow night it is Harry Belafonte. The first clue to the state of the box office for the LSO and Classic Rock is that no one quite knows how many people the stadium holds. When a concert is sold out, everyone knows to the last ticket, how many seats there are.

The Classic Rock management team are trying bravely to foster excitement, some sense of 'an event'. Someone has thought to order witty T-shirts each with its own inscription on the back: 'Gothenburg, Classic Rock '83. Where the hell is Rafael Ravenscroft' – or Tony Prior, or Richard Harvey, John Kurlander etc. There is even one that reads 'Where the hell is Carl Bernestierna?' ('Who the hell is he?' asks an LSO principal.) He is the man from Skandia Insurance who is sponsoring tonight's concert. This sponsorship is a considerable coup and before the night is over, various people will be scrambling to assume responsibility for it. In times like this, everyone wants to be known as 'a rainmaker', the one who makes the money fall.

The point is that in all this jolly pulling-together of the lads who matter, someone forgot to take the LSO into account. No shirt for Anthony Camden, no dip of the knee to tonight's LSO leader, Ashley Arbuckle. The LSO talks of hiring itself out, rather as if it were a marquee or a hotel ballroom. It does not like the reality much. The joke is that this is an LSO concert as much as it is anyone's, but there is a disquieting feeling of having been taken over and occupied. It is one thing to complain of not controlling your own artistic destiny because some conductor wants to take a movement too fast. It is another to be microphone fodder.

John Kurlander's mikes are slowly lining up: a lead in here, a connection over there. A gigantic battery of oversized speakers hangs above the orchestra pointing forward. Behind these speakers, fortunately, the sound is almost enchantingly tinkly. In front of them, it besieges the ears ferociously. The development of speakers such as these has been a nightmare and a curse on classical music: who, in years to come, will find passion and drama in the sound of the symphony orchestra after tasting the power of electric decibels? Most great classical music was written to be played in a small space – a court room, a ballroom at the most. It is rooted in the idea of intimate listening. This is another dimension.

A violinist may pay a quarter of a million pounds to buy a wooden box, two or three hundred years old, because he believes that the greatness of a certain old maker will give him more tone, more resonance, more power. How ironic it is: one of those speakers hanging in the air above the LSO could in itself drown out 20 of the greatest Stradivari violins or simply alter their character beyond recognition.

'An echo, an echo, have you got the echo?', someone calls somewhere. 'The flutes are very quiet,' someone else advises the electronic wizard, John Kurlander; as if he cannot hear it for himself. Kurlander is magnificent this afternoon; he is a virtuoso. He is the one man here who has everything in common with the best orchestra players: he is striving for an ideal sound. There is a kind of perfectionism that drives him. He stands behind his console, tugging on an ear, tense, fanatical. He is surrounded by hundreds of switches, buttons, raisers, levellers and mixers and his concentration is absolute. For once the orchestra is truly an instrument upon which one man plays. Next to him, the most inspired conductor is but a Shaman. Tonight Kurlander is actually making the sound.

By the time the rehearsal ends at six, there is an hour and a half to gulp a coffee and sandwich in the backstage cafeteria before going off to change into tails. There is a most inconvenient current of cold air whipping around the stadium at ankle level. It is bleak. A symphony orchestra is a museum piece, a collector's item. It does not feel at its best, its most expansive out here in the modern world. Standing on rubber pads over an ice rink, playing with ear stops to cushion the noise, is not the way they teach it at the Royal Academy of Music.

Comfortingly in the midst of everything, some aspects of life never change; they reassuringly carry on regardless. In the cafeteria, spread over a table, Sue Mallet confronts her 'brains' while she and John Duffy, the personnel manager, get down to some long-term planning and short-term odds and ends. Sue has been on the telephone as usual leaving messages on various answer phones in various countries across three continents. Do they have string strength for *Pulcinella* next week? The RCA recording sessions for John Corigliano's flute concerto are 'really shaking like blazes' and the film sessions are off. But the Heinz Baked Beans children's competition is going to be worth at least two sessions and there is a possibility of recording the music for an ice show in America. Dorking is confirmed for a concert and Paris is looking good. It will be the basic Mahler One – the touring version, the skeleton, providing of course that Claudio does not get wind of it. Claudio has already stipulated ten double basses for Paris. 'Can't afford it,' says Sue firmly. 'It has to be eight.' Claudio does not like the orchestra having to take so much commercial work. There are certain things he does like and most of them cost money. A Classic Rock pays for many artistic luxuries. 'We're very versatile,' says John Duffy cheerily, 'we'll turn our hand to anything.' They have to; most collectors' items do not live, breathe and have families to keep.

Thursday morning

It is five thirty in the morning. Somehow Sue Mallet has persuaded the management of the Hotel Opalen to set up a breakfast buffet for the orchestra. A surprising number of musicians have made the effort to get down early enough for the juice, coffee and rolls. Playing together and going out at night on tour is one thing; this grey-faced, unguarded moment before dawn is the true intimacy of living together. The smokers with their early, sticky coughs; the ones who look much older and pudgier than they like others to know; the big bad boys who look more open and gentle before the craftiness within gets going.

The regular poker set probably never went to bed. A few, who must always be such early risers, are like moles quivering with the newness of the day. Bill Lang, smooth and pink, has even had a shave. For all the banter, they hold one another very dear. It is why the one or two odd men out, whom no one likes too well, seem so isolated as they sit busying themselves with butter, rolls and jam. When everyone is too sleepy still to pretend or to cover up, affection is, as the LSO likes to say, 'on the table, giving it one'. The yawns, the scratching, the foggy chests and hangovers: they have known one another through many dawns like this.

The concert is hardly spoken of. It was not their success, really. The stadium was about a third full, the amplification was stunning, if you like that kind of thing – and 5000 or so people seemingly did (5000: a small gate for a pop concert and two full Barbican halls' worth. It is an absurd thought). Richard Harvey discovered a talent for being droll and fey in an English, John Cleese-ish kind of way and the Swedes enjoyed him. There was a party afterwards to which the whole orchestra was invited. It was in a crowded, vaulted reception room at the top of a cold and winding stone staircase. Outside in the hallway was a line of imposing portraits: Fredrik Åkerblom 1839-1901, F.M. Colliander 1827-1914, their credentials for being so honoured unfathomable to the visitors. It was not a place to feel at home, and the news that drinks would have to be paid for confirmed that it would be a quiet and early night. A few stagger down into the hotel lobby only seconds before the coaches leave for the airport but theirs were private nights, some haunted, some thrown carelessly away as the still hours passed.

Landvetter Airport is almost empty; a plane or two stands outside on the tarmac. The sound of the LSO shuffling up to immigration and security and of overstuffed shoulder bags being dragged behind along the hard floor is a familiar theme, echoing back down the hallway. More cups of black coffee are hastily and thankfully swallowed before the plane's departure is announced.

This is no celebration: there is no fire, there are no regrets. It is the London Symphony Orchestra doing its job competently and going home again. There is no privacy on tour. The lasting image of the LSO is of the backs of a small crowd of people filing through departure gates all over the world. They know each other too well for there to be awkward jostling or pushing; they are so attuned by now that they do not even bother to watch out for bags or feet or violin cases; one hundred or so individuals held together closely enough that they can move as one.

It seems dreary at Victoria Station when the train from Gatwick Airport finally arrives in London. All those faces, now so familiar, just melt away. In one instant, those huge figures full of life shrink and vanish in the crowd. 'Going back to the normal world' is the way they put it in the orchestra. It is lonely, though, without the chaps.

12: Epilogue

London, Sunday evening

Outside the artists' entrance of the Royal Festival Hall there are two large vans. The Royal Philharmonic Orchestra is on its way out; the London Symphony Orchestra is on its way in. Douglas Davenport, the burly LSO driver, one-time driving instructor and former furniture remover, arrived back from Gothenburg a few hours ago. Tonight there is the Brahms German Requiem; he has two hours to unload the instruments and get them on the lift upstairs and on to the stage. 'The only fear we've got is if other people give us a hand.' It never stops, the movement from one place to another, one concert to another.

It is a week since the LSO last played the Brahms with Abbado. It is going into tonight's concert without a run-through; some musicians cannot have touched their instruments since they left them to be loaded up backstage after Thursday night's Classic Rock. Fortunately, Claudio has forgotten that the orchestra had to go to Gothenburg and back after he last saw them or, doubtless, there would have been a long and exacting rehearsal this morning.

Upstairs in the bar before the concert the atmosphere is subdued. Duggie Cummings is at home recuperating. Ashley Arbuckle, co-leader, left for Florida on Thursday for a chamber music tour. Osian Ellis has been told to take two months off because of exhaustion. And Donald Stewart, the gentle Scots violinist, died on Friday.

On the general bulletin board at the Festival Hall, there are notices galore: memorial services for young musicians, scholarships endowed in the name of talented cancer victims. Someone is heard to mention that one of the Philharmonia Orchestra's best horns may never play again. The section, it is said, was driving back from the Edinburgh Festival too fast and too late. There was an accident. 'You'd think everyone would know about doing that – how can they be so bloody stupid?' asks Tony Chidell, chilled by this latest tragedy. Denis Brain died in such a crash.

On a more prosaic, everyday level, the board is full of tales of woe, of instruments lost and stolen. Martin Gatt, the LSO principal bassoon, has posted a long list of instruments – almost his entire collection was stolen in a burglary. There are violas that disappeared from cars; violins that went missing in hotel rooms – and only a hint of the most distressing of all losses, the bows that somehow vanish backstage in concert halls. Before the concert,

Norman Clarke and William Brown, *Usher Hall, Edinburgh*

late this afternoon, Anthony Camden held a full shareholders' meeting to lay before the members the whole worrying financial picture. There seems to be no respite.

At 7.30, nevertheless, the LSO is on stage. Who would guess the sadnesses and concerns behind those black-and-white uniformed figures sitting so calmly before the conductor comes out? The Royal Festival Hall is not sold out, but it is a good house tonight. The excellent reviews last week and word of mouth must have helped. From where the audience sits, it seems like just another LSO concert, just as it has always seemed for nearly eight years. It looks no different from the front than it ever does. How many concertgoers, even the enthusiasts, sit and count the missing faces? There are no empty chairs; somehow, someone always does the job.

The soloists for the Requiem come out. Margaret Marshall from Stirling and Hermann Prey from Berlin ushered on by Claudio Abbado from Milan. They look as gracious and imposing as such stars always do. Would it have been nice to say a word or two beforehand, to dedicate this music, perhaps, to Donald Stewart? Perhaps it is inappropriate and in any case many of his colleagues will be playing in his memory tonight, seeing him in their mind's eye with his inevitable cigarette and wry smile.

A year before Brahms started to sketch this Requiem, his friend and mentor, Robert Schumann had died in intense mental and spiritual agony. The tragedy and anguish of those lives have meaning to us now only through the heartfelt majesty of this music. Death, glory, redemption and life: these are eternal considerations. No man can live constantly in their shadow, just as no musician can play constantly from his deepest passion.

There are people who will barely be able to stay awake through the six movements or to conceal their boredom. Some will say that the performance was dull, the orchestra not on form or the singers not exciting enough. But there are also people who will, when the concert ends, have tears in their eyes. Some of them will immediately shake their heads crossly as if caught in some act of utter foolishness. Others might, for a few brief moments, feel as if they have been transformed and gratefuly welcome that sensation. Music has that power sometimes; those who earn their living by it never quite forget that, never quite overcome their awe before the greatest composers.

Backstage afterwards the usual well-dressed crowd surrounds the soloists' and conductor's dressing rooms. Doubtless the same elegance will be on view next month when Claudio conducts a new production of *Boris Godunov* at the Royal Opera House, Covent Garden. At the other end of the backstage corridor Jenny, the fourth chair cellist, sits in the bar, patiently waiting to collect her father Jim Brown. She is back from holiday and could not stay away. 'I missed them all,' she says. 'It's called "pining for the lads". I'm so knocked out by all these people – I don't think I could ever marry anyone else outside an orchestra.'

Colleagues drop in to admire her tan, to ask about Greece and mainly to let her know that they are glad she is back. 'Perhaps I have gone overboard on this lot but this orchestra matters to me more than anything else in the world. My terror is to end up 45 and clapped out, lonely, superseded by beautiful young lady cellists and playing Tchaikovsky nights at the Albert Hall. Occasionally the odd twinge of panic or just of boredom sets in and then I remind myself of where I am and who I am playing with. I look round at them and they are all my heroes. How many people doing a job can say that?'

Anthony Camden has promised to read this book in manuscript. He has agreed to correct the facts; the opinions are not his to correct. He reads it through and for some time will not discuss it. When he does, he tries to explain something that is hard for him to put into words: 'It may be fair,' he says reluctantly, 'but when I look around at my colleagues and when I think of the LSO – and I'm not talking about me but of *them* and of *it* – well, I have always thought and I do really think that it is much more exciting than it reads here.' It is the best tribute anyone or anything could have: to mean so much to those who are part of it.